"What are you doing here?"

"I had to see you. I'm sorry it took me so long. Could we talk?"

Chase.

Mary felt heat rush to her center. The cowboy standing in front of her set off all kinds of desires with only a look. And yet after all this time, did she know this man?

"I got your letter," he said as he took off his Stetson, turning the brim nervously in his fingers.

"You didn't call or write back."

His gaze locked with hers. "What I wanted to say couldn't be said over the phone, let alone in a letter."

Her heart pounded. *Here it comes.*

There was pain in his gaze. "I've missed you so much. I had to go. Just as I had to come back. I'm so sorry I hurt you." His blue-eyed gaze locked with hers. "I love you. I never stopped loving you."

Wasn't this exactly what she'd dreamed of him saying to her before she'd gotten the call from his fiancée?

Except in the dream she would have been in his arms by now...

STEEL RESOLVE

New York Times Bestselling Author
B.J. DANIELS

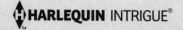

This one is for Terry Scones, who always brightens my day. I laugh when I recall a quilt shop hop we made across Montana. She was the navigator when my GPS system tried to send us through a barn.

ISBN-13: 978-1-335-60445-3

Steel Resolve

Copyright © 2019 by Barbara Heinlein

Recycling programs for this product may not exist in your area.

Printed in U.S.A.

www.Harlequin.com

B.J. Daniels is a *New York Times* and *USA TODAY* bestselling author. She wrote her first book after a career as an award-winning newspaper journalist and author of thirty-seven published short stories. She lives in Montana with her husband, Parker, and three springer spaniels. When not writing, she quilts, boats and plays tennis. Contact her at bjdaniels.com, on Facebook or on Twitter, @bjdanielsauthor.

Books by B.J. Daniels

Harlequin Intrigue

Cardwell Ranch: Montana Legacy

Steel Resolve

Whitehorse, Montana: The Clementine Sisters

Hard Rustler
Rogue Gunslinger
Rugged Defender

The Montana Cahills

Cowboy's Redemption

Whitehorse, Montana: The McGraw Kidnapping

Dark Horse
Dead Ringer
Rough Rider

HQN Books

Sterling's Montana

Stroke of Luck
Luck of the Draw

The Montana Cahills

Renegade's Pride
Outlaw's Honor
Hero's Return
Rancher's Dream

Visit the Author Profile page at Harlequin.com.

CAST OF CHARACTERS

Chase Steele—The cowboy gave up the woman he loved and has regretted it ever since. But maybe it isn't too late...if he can get back to Montana alive.

Mary Cardwell Savage—Her life was in danger the moment she mailed the letter to Chase telling him she still loved him.

Fiona Barkley—The moment she saw Chase Steele she was determined this was the man she would marry. And she wasn't going to let anyone come between them.

Lucy Carson—She would do anything—anything at all—to be Mary's friend.

Dillon Ramsey—He has his own reasons for wanting to date the marshal's daughter.

Marshal Hud Savage—All he wants is for his daughter to be happy, but why, when it comes to men, does she pick the wild ones?

Dana Cardwell Savage—She knows the man her daughter should choose. But it seems something—or someone—is trying to keep them apart.

Chapter One

The moment Fiona found the letter in the bottom of Chase's sock drawer, she knew it was bad news. Fear squeezed the breath from her as her heart beat so hard against her rib cage that she thought she would pass out. Grabbing the bureau for support, she told herself it might not be what she thought it was.

But the envelope was a pale lavender, and the handwriting was distinctly female. Worse, Chase had kept the letter a secret. Why else would it be hidden under his socks? He hadn't wanted her to see it because it was from that other woman.

Now she wished she hadn't been snooping around. She'd let herself into his house with the extra key she'd had made. She'd felt him pulling away from her the past few weeks. Having been here so many times before, she was determined that this one wasn't going to break her heart. Nor was she going to let another woman take him from her. That's why she had to find out why he hadn't called, why he wasn't returning her messages, why he was avoiding her.

They'd had fun the night they were together. She'd felt as if they had something special, although she knew the next morning that he was feeling guilty. He'd said he didn't want to lead her on. He'd told her that there was some woman back home he was still in love with. He'd said their night together was a mistake. But he was wrong, and she was determined to convince him of it.

What made it so hard was that Chase was a genuinely nice guy. You didn't let a man like that get away. The other woman had. Fiona wasn't going to make that mistake even though he'd been trying to push her away since that night. But he had no idea how determined she could be, determined enough for both of them that this wasn't over by a long shot.

It wasn't the first time she'd let herself into his apartment when he was at work. The other time, he'd caught her and she'd had to make up some story about the building manager letting her in so she could look for her lost earring.

She'd snooped around his house the first night they'd met—the same night she'd found his extra apartment key and had taken it to have her own key made in case she ever needed to come back when Chase wasn't home.

The letter hadn't been in his sock drawer that time.

That meant he'd received it since then. Hadn't she known he was hiding something from her? Why else would he put this letter in a drawer instead of leaving it out along with the bills he'd casually dropped on the table by the front door?

Because the letter was important to him, which meant that she had no choice but to read it.

Her heart compressed into a hard knot as she carefully lifted out the envelope. The handwriting made her pulse begin to roar in her ears. The woman's handwriting was very neat, very precise. She hated her immediately. The return address confirmed it. The letter was from the woman back in Montana that Chase had told her he was still in love with.

Mary Cardwell Savage, the woman who'd broken Chase's heart and one of the reasons that the cowboy had ended up in Arizona. Her friend Patty told her all about him. Chase worked for her husband, Rick. That's how she and Chase had met, at a party at their house.

What struck her now was the date on the postmark. Her vision blurred for a moment. *Two weeks ago?* Anger flared inside her again. That was right after their night together. About the same time that he'd gotten busy and didn't have time, he said, to date or even talk. What had this woman said in her letter? Whatever it was, Fiona knew it was the cause of the problem with her and Chase.

Her fingers trembled as she carefully opened the envelope flap and slipped out the folded sheet of pale lavender paper. The color alone made her sick to her stomach. She sniffed it, half expecting to smell the woman's perfume.

There was only a faint scent, just enough to be disturbing. She listened for a moment, afraid Chase might come home early and catch her again. He'd been angry the last time. He would be even more furious if he caught her reading the letter he'd obviously hidden from her.

Unfolding the sheet of paper she tried to brace herself. She felt as if her entire future hung on what was inside this envelope.

Her throat closed as she read the words, devouring them as quickly as her gaze could take them in. After only a few sentences, she let her gaze drop to the bottom line, her heart dropping with it: *I'll always love you, Mary.*

This was the woman Chase said he was still in love with. She'd broken up with him and now she wanted him back? Who did this Mary Savage of Big Sky, Montana, think she was? Fury churned inside Fiona as she quickly read all the way through the letter, the words breaking her heart and filling her with an all-consuming rage.

Mary Savage had apparently pretended that she was only writing to Chase to let him know that some friend of his mother's had dropped by with a package for him. If he confirmed his address, she'd be happy to send the package if he was interested.

But after that, the letter had gotten personal. Fiona stared at the words, fury warring with heartbreaking pain. The package was clearly only a ruse for the rest of the letter, which was a sickening attempt to lure him back. This woman was still in love with Chase. It made her sick to read the words that were such an obvious effort to remind him of their love, first love, and all that included. This woman had history with Chase. She missed him and regretted the way they'd left things. The woman had even included her phone number. In case he'd forgotten it?

Had Chase called her? The thought sent a wave

of nausea through her, followed quickly by growing vehemence. She couldn't believe this. *This woman was not taking Chase away from her!* She wouldn't allow it. She and Chase had only gotten started, but Fiona knew that he was perfect for her and she for him. If anyone could help him get over this other woman, it was her. Chase was hers now. She would just have to make him see that.

Fiona tried to calm herself. The worst thing she could do was to confront Chase and demand to know why he had kept this from her. She didn't need him to remind her that they didn't have "that kind" of relationship as he had the other times. Not to mention how strained things had been between them lately. She'd felt him pulling away and had called and stopped by at every opportunity, afraid she was losing him.

And now she knew why. If the woman had been in Arizona, she would have gone to her house and— Deep breaths, she told herself. She had to calm down. She had to remember what had happened the last time. She'd almost ended up in jail.

Taking deep breaths, she reminded herself that this woman was no threat. Mary Cardwell Savage wasn't in Arizona. She lived in Montana, hundreds of miles away.

But that argument did nothing to relieve her wrath or her growing apprehension. Chase hadn't just kept the letter. He'd *hidden* it. His little *secret*. And worse, he was avoiding her, trying to give her the brush-off. She felt herself hyperventilating.

She knew she had to stop this. She thought of

how good things had been between her and Chase that first night. The cowboy was so incredibly sexy, and he'd remarked how lovely she looked in her tailored suit and heels. He'd complimented her long blond hair as he unpinned it and let it fall around her shoulders. When he'd looked into her green eyes, she hadn't needed him to tell her that he loved her. She had seen it.

The memory made her smile. And he'd enjoyed what she had waiting for him underneath that suit— just as she knew he would. They'd both been a little drunk that night. She'd had to make all the moves, but she hadn't minded.

Not that she would ever admit it to him, but she'd set her sights on him the moment she'd seen him at the party. There was something about him that had drawn her. A vulnerability she recognized. He'd been hurt before. So had she, too many times to count. She'd told herself that the handsome cowboy didn't know just how perfect he was, perfect for her.

Fiona hadn't exactly thrown herself at him. She'd just been determined to make him forget that other woman by making herself indispensable. She'd brought over dinner the next night. He'd been too polite to turn her away. She'd come up with things they could do together: baseball games, picnics, movies. But the harder she'd tried, the more he'd made excuses for why he couldn't go with her.

She stared down at the letter still in her hands, wanting to rip it to shreds, to tear this woman's eyes out, to—

Suddenly she froze. Was that the door of the apart-

ment opening? It was. Just as she'd feared, Chase had
come home early.

At the sound of the door closing and locking, she
hurriedly refolded the letter, slipped it back into the
envelope and shoved it under his socks. She was
trapped. There was no way to get out of the apartment without him seeing her. He was going to be
upset with her. But the one thing she couldn't let
Chase know was that she'd found and read the letter. She couldn't give him an excuse to break things
off indefinitely, even though she knew he'd been trying to do just that for the past couple of weeks—ever
since he'd gotten that letter.

She hurried to the bedroom door, but hesitated.
Maybe she should get naked and let him find her
lying on his bed. She wasn't sure she could pull that
off right now. Standing there, she tried to swallow
back the anger, the hurt, the fear. She couldn't let him
know what she was feeling—let alone how desperate
she felt. But as she heard him coming up the stairs,
she had a terrifying thought.

What if she'd put the letter back in the drawer
wrong? Had she seen the woman's handwriting on
the envelope? Wasn't that why she'd felt such a jolt?
Or was it just seeing the pale lavender paper of the
envelope in his sock drawer that had made her realize what it was?

She couldn't remember.

But would Chase remember how he'd left it and
know that she'd seen it? Know that if she'd found it,
she would read it?

She glanced back and saw that she hadn't closed

the top dresser drawer all the way. Hurrying back over to it, she shut the drawer as quietly as possible and was about to turn when she heard him in the doorway.

"Fiona? What the hell?" He looked startled at first when he saw her, and then shock quickly turned to anger.

She could see that she'd scared him. He'd scared her too. Her heart was a drum in her chest. She was clearly rattled. She could feel the fine mist of perspiration on her upper lip. With one look, he would know something was wrong.

But how could she not be upset? The man she'd planned to marry had kept a letter from his ex a secret from her. Worse, the woman he'd been pining over when Fiona had met him was still in love with him—and now he knew it. Hiding the letter proved that he was at least thinking about Mary Cardwell Savage.

"What are you doing here?" Chase demanded, glancing around as if the answer was in the room. "How the hell did you get in *this* time?"

She tried to cover, letting out an embarrassed laugh. "You startled me. I was looking for my favorite lipstick. I thought I might have left it here."

He shook his head, raking a hand through his hair. "You have to stop this. I told you last time. Fiona—" His blue gaze swept past her to light on the chest of drawers.

Any question as to how he felt about the letter was quickly answered by his protective glance toward the top bureau drawer and the letter from his first love, the young woman who'd broken his tender heart, the woman he was still in love with.

Her own heart broke, shattering like a glass thrown against a wall. She wanted to kill Mary Cardwell Savage.

"Your lipstick?" He shook his head. "Again, how did you get in here?"

"You forgot to lock your door. I came by hoping to catch your building manager so he could let me in again—"

"Fiona, stop lying. I talked to him after the last time. He didn't let you in." The big cowboy held out his hand. "Give it to me."

She pretended not to know what he was talking about, blinking her big green eyes at him in the best innocent look she could muster. She couldn't lose this man. She wouldn't. She did the only thing she could. She reached into her pocket and pulled out the key. "I can explain."

"No need," he said as he took the key.

She felt real tears of remorse fill her eyes. But she saw that he was no longer affected by her tears. She stepped to him to put her arms around his neck and pulled him down for a kiss. Maybe if she could draw him toward the bed…

"Fiona, stop." He grabbed her wrists and pulled them from around his neck. *"Stop!"*

She stared at him, feeling the happy life she'd planned crumbling under her feet.

He groaned and shook his head. "You need to leave."

"Sure," she said and, trying to get control of her

emotions, started to step past him. "Just let me look in one more place for my lipstick. I know I had it—"

"No," he said, blocking her way. "Your lipstick isn't here and we both know it. Just like your phone wasn't here the last time you stopped by. This has to stop. I don't want to see you again."

"You don't mean that." Her voice broke. "Is this about the letter from that bitch who dumped you?"

His gaze shot to the bureau again. She watched his expression change from frustrated to furious. "You've been going through my things?"

"I told you, I was looking for my lipstick. I'm sorry I found the letter. You hadn't called, and I thought maybe it was because of the letter."

He sighed, and when he spoke it was as if he was talking to a small unruly child. "Fiona, I told you from the first night we met that I wasn't ready for another relationship. You caught me at a weak moment, otherwise nothing would have happened between the two of us. I'd had too much to drink, and my boss's wife insisted that I let you drive me back to my apartment." He groaned. "I'm not trying to make excuses for what happened. We are both adults. But I was honest with you." He looked pained, his blue eyes dark. "I'm sorry if you thought that that night was more than it was. But now you have to leave and not come back."

"We can't be over! You have to give me another chance." She'd heard the words before from other men, more times than she wanted to remember. "I'm sorry. I was wrong to come here when you weren't home. I won't do anything like this again. I promise."

"Stop!" he snapped. "You're not listening. Look," he said, lowering his voice. "You might as well know that I'm leaving at the end of the week. My job here is over."

"Leaving?" This couldn't be happening. "Where are you going?" she cried, and felt her eyes widen in alarm. "You're going back to Montana. *Back to her.* Mary Cardwell Savage." She spit out the words as if they were stones that had been lodged in her throat.

He shook his head. "I told you the night we met that there was no chance of me falling for another woman because I was still in love with someone else."

She sneered at him. "She broke your heart. She'll do it again. Don't let her. She's nobody." She took a step toward him. "I can make you happy if you'll just give me a chance."

"Fiona, please go before either of us says something we'll regret," Chase said in a tone she'd never heard from him before. He was shutting her out. For good.

If he would only let her kiss him… She reached for him, thinking she could make him remember what they had together, but he pushed her back.

"Don't." He was shaking his head, looking at her as if horrified by her. There was anguish in his gaze. But there was also pity and disgust. That too she'd seen before. She felt a dark shell close around her heart.

"You'll be sorry," she said, feeling crushed but at the same time infused with a cold, murderous fury.

"I should have never have let this happen," Chase was saying. "This is all my fault. I'm so sorry."

Oh, he didn't know sorry, but he would soon enough. He would rue this day. And if he thought he'd seen the last of her, he was in for a surprise. That Montana hayseed would have Chase over her dead body.

Chapter Two

"I feel terrible that I didn't warn you about Fiona," his boss said on Chase's last day of work. Rick had insisted on buying him a beer after quitting time.

Now in the cool dark of the bar, Chase looked at the man and said, "So she's done this before?"

Rick sighed. "She gets attached if a man pays any attention to her in the least and can't let go, but don't worry, she'll meet some other guy and get crazy over him. It's a pattern with her. She and my wife went to high school together. Patty feels sorry for her and keeps hoping she'll meet someone and settle down."

Chase shook his head, remembering his first impression of the woman. Fiona had seemed so together, so…normal. She sold real estate, dressed like a polished professional and acted like one. She'd come up to him at a barbecue at Rick's house. Chase hadn't wanted to go, but his boss had insisted, saying it would do him good to get out more.

He'd just lost his mother. His mother, Muriel, had been sick for some time. It was one of the reasons he'd come to Arizona in the first place. The other was that he knew he could find work here as a carpenter. Muriel had made him promise that when she died, he would take her ashes back to Montana. He'd been with her at the end, hoping that she would finally tell him the one thing she'd kept from him all these years. But she hadn't. She'd taken her secret to the grave and left him with more questions than answers—and an urn full of her ashes.

"You need to get out occasionally," Rick had said when Chase left work to go pick up the urn from the mortuary. It was in a velvet bag. He'd stuffed it behind the seat of his pickup on the way to the barbecue.

"All you do is work, then hide out in your apartment not to be seen again until you do the same thing the next day," Rick had argued. "You might just have fun and I cook damned good barbecue. Come on, it's just a few friends."

He'd gone, planning not to stay longer than it took to drink a couple of beers and have some barbecued ribs. He'd been on his second beer when he'd seen her. Fiona stood out among the working-class men and women at the party because she'd come straight from her job at a local real estate company.

She wore high heels that made her long legs look even longer. Her curvaceous body was molded into a dark suit with a white blouse and gold jewelry. Her long blond hair was pulled up, accentuating her tanned throat against the white of her blouse.

He'd become intensely aware of how long it had been since he'd felt anything but anguish over his breakup with Mary and his mother's sickness, and the secret that she'd taken with her.

"Fiona Barkley," she'd said, extending her hand.

Her hand had been cool and dry, her grip strong. "Chase Steele."

She'd chuckled, her green eyes sparking with humor. "For real? A cowboy named Chase Steele?"

"My father was an extra in a bunch of Western movies," he lied since he had no idea who his father had been.

She cocked a brow at him. "Really?"

He shook his head. "I grew up on a ranch in Montana." He shrugged. "Cowboying is in my blood."

Fiona had taken his almost empty beer can from him and handed him her untouched drink. "Try that. I can tell that you need it." The drink had been strong and buzzed through his bloodstream.

Normally she wasn't the type of woman he gravitated toward. But she was so different from Mary, and it had been so long since he'd even thought about another woman. The party atmosphere, the urn behind his pickup seat and the drinks Fiona kept plying him with added to his what-the-hell attitude that night.

"How long have you two been dating?" Rick asked now in the cool dark of the bar.

"We never dated. I told her that first night that I was in love with someone else. But I made the mistake of sleeping with her. Sleeping with anyone given the way I feel about the woman back home was a mistake."

"So you told Fiona there was another woman." His boss groaned. "That explains a lot. Fiona now sees it as a competition between her and the other woman.

She won't give up. She hates losing. It's what makes her such a great Realtor."

"Well, it's all moot now since I'm leaving for Montana."

Rick didn't look convinced that it would be that easy. "Does she know?"

He nodded.

"Well, hopefully you'll get out of town without any trouble."

"Thanks a lot."

"Sorry, but according to Patty, when Fiona feels the man pulling away… Well, it makes her a little… crazy."

Chase shook his head. "This just keeps getting better and better." He picked up his beer, drained it and got to his feet. "I'm going home to pack. The sooner I get out of town the better."

"I wish I could talk you out of leaving," Rick said. "You're one of the best finish carpenters I've had in a long time. I hope you're not leaving because of Fiona. Seriously, she'll latch on to someone else. I wouldn't worry about it. It's just Fiona being Fiona. Unless you're going back to this woman you're in love with?"

He laughed. "If only it were that easy. She's the one who broke it off with me." He liked Rick. But the man hadn't warned him about Fiona, and if Rick mentioned to Patty who mentioned to Fiona… He knew he was being overly cautious. Fiona wouldn't follow him all the way to Montana. She had a job, a condo, a life here. But still, he found himself saying,

"Not sure what I'm doing. Might stop off in Colorado for a while."

"Well, good luck. And again, sorry about Fiona."

As he left the bar, he thought about Mary and the letter he'd hidden in his sock drawer with her phone number. He'd thought about calling her to let her know he was headed home. He was also curious about the package she'd said a friend of his mother had left for him.

Since getting the letter, he'd thought about calling dozens of times. But what he had to say, he couldn't in a phone call. He had to see Mary. Now that he was leaving, he couldn't wait to hit the road.

MARY CARDWELL SAVAGE reined in her horse to look out at the canyon below her. The Gallatin River wound through rugged cliffs and stands of pines, the water running clear over the colored rocks as pale green aspen leaves winked from the shore. Beyond the river and the trees, she could make out the resort town that had sprouted up across the canyon. She breathed in the cool air rich with the scent of pine and the crisp cool air rising off the water.

Big Sky, Montana, had changed so much in her lifetime and even more in her mother's. Dana Cardwell Savage had seen the real changes after the ski resort had been built at the foot of Lone Peak. Big Sky had gone from a ranching community to a resort area, and finally to a town with a whole lot of housing developments and businesses rising to the community's growing needs.

The growth had meant more work for her father,

Marshal Hud Savage. He'd been threatening to retire since he said he no longer recognized the canyon community anymore. More deputies had to be hired each year because the area was experiencing more crime.

Just the thought of the newest deputy who'd been hired made her smile a little. Dillon Ramsey was the kind of man a woman noticed—even one who had given her heart away when she was fifteen and had never gotten it back.

Dillon, with his dark wavy hair and midnight black eyes, had asked her out, and she'd said she'd think about it. If her best friend Kara had been around, she would have thought Mary had lost her mind. Anyone who saw Dillon knew two things about him. He was a hunk, and he was dangerous to the local female population.

Since telling him she'd think about it, she had been mentally kicking herself. Had she really been sitting around waiting to hear from Chase? What was wrong with her? It had been weeks. When she'd broken it off and sent him packing, she hadn't been sitting around moping over him. Not really. She'd been busy starting a career, making a life for herself. So what had made her write that stupid letter?

Wasn't it obvious that if he'd gotten her letter, he should have called by now? Since the letter hadn't come back, she had to assume that it had arrived just fine. The fact that he hadn't called or written her back meant that he wasn't interested. He also must not be interested in the package his mother's friend had left for him either. It was high time to forget about that cowboy, and why not do it with Dillon Ramsey?

Because she couldn't quit thinking about Chase and hadn't been able to since she'd first laid eyes on him when they were both fifteen. They'd been inseparable all through high school and college. Four years ago he'd told her he was going to have to leave. They'd both been twenty-four, too young to settle down, according to her father and Chase had agreed. He needed to go find himself since not knowing who his father was still haunted him.

It had broken her heart when he'd left her—and Montana. She'd dated little after he left town. Mostly because she'd found herself comparing the men she had dated to Chase. At least with Dillon, she sensed a wild, dangerousness in him that appealed to her right now.

Her father hadn't liked hearing that Dillon had asked her out. "I wish you'd reconsider," he'd said when she'd stopped by Cardwell Ranch where she'd grown up. She'd bought her own place in Meadow Village closer to the center of town, and made the first floor into her office. On the third floor was her apartment where she lived. The second floor had been made into one-bedroom apartments that she rented.

But she still spent a lot of time on the ranch because that's where her heart was—her family, her horses and her love for the land. She hadn't even gone far away to college—just forty miles to Montana State University in Bozeman. She couldn't be far from Cardwell Ranch and couldn't imagine that she ever would. She was her mother's daughter, she thought. Cardwell Ranch was her legacy.

Dana Cardwell had fought for this ranch years ago when her brothers and sister had wanted to sell it and split the money after their mother died. Dana couldn't bear to part with the family ranch. Fortunately, her grandmother, Mary Cardwell, had left Dana the ranch in her last will, knowing Dana would keep the place in the family always.

Ranching had been in her grandmother's blood, the woman Mary had been named after. Just as it was in Dana's and now Mary's. Chase hadn't understood why she couldn't walk away from this legacy that the women in her family had fought so hard for.

But while her mother was a hands-on ranch woman, Mary liked working behind the scenes. She'd taken over the accounting part of running the ranch so her mother could enjoy what she loved— being on the back of a horse.

"What is wrong with Dillon Ramsey?" Dana Cardwell Savage had asked her husband after Mary had told them that the deputy had asked her out.

"He's new and, if you must know, there's something troublesome about him that I haven't been able to put my finger on yet," Hud had said.

Mary had laughed. She knew exactly what bothered her father about Dillon—the same thing that attracted her to the young cocky deputy. If she couldn't have Chase, then why not take a walk on the wild side for once?

She had just finished unsaddling her horse and was headed for the main house when her cell phone rang, startling her. Her pulse jumped. She dug the phone out and looked at the screen, her heart in her throat. It was a long-distance number and not one she recognized. Chase?

Sure took him long enough to finally call, she thought, and instantly found herself making excuses for him. Maybe he was working away from cell phone coverage. It happened all the time in Montana. Why not in Arizona? Or maybe her letter had to chase him down, and he'd just now gotten it and called the moment he read it.

It rang a second time. She swallowed the lump in her throat. She couldn't believe how nervous she was. Silly goose, she thought. It's probably not Chase at all but some telemarketer calling to try to sell her something.

She answered on the third ring. "Hello?" Her voice cracked.

Silence, then a female voice. "Mary Cardwell Savage?" The voice was hard and crisp like a fall apple, the words bitten off.

"Yes?" she asked, disappointed. She'd gotten her hopes up that it was Chase, with whatever excuse he had for not calling sooner. It wouldn't matter as long as he'd called to say that he felt the same way she did and always had. But she'd been right. It was just some telemarketer. "I'm sorry, but whatever you're selling, I'm not inter—"

"I read your letter you sent Chase."

Her breath caught as her heart missed a beat. She told herself that she'd heard wrong. "I beg your pardon?"

"Leave my fiancé alone. Don't write him. Don't call him. Just leave him the hell alone."

She tried to swallow around the bitter taste in her mouth. "Who is this?" Her voice sounded breathy with fear.

"The woman who's going to marry Chase Steele. If you ever contact him again—"

Mary disconnected, her fingers trembling as she dropped the phone into her jacket pocket as if it had scorched her skin. The woman's harsh low voice was still in her ears, furious and threatening. Whoever she was, she'd read the letter. No wonder Chase hadn't written or called. But why hadn't he? Had he shown the letter to his fiancée? Torn it up? Kept it so she found it? Did it matter? His fiancée had read the letter and was furious, and Mary couldn't blame her.

She buried her face in her hands. Chase had gone off to find himself. Apparently he'd succeeded in finding a fiancée as well. Tears burned her eyes. Chase was engaged and getting married. Could she be a bigger fool? Chase had moved on, and he hadn't even had the guts to call and tell her.

Angrily, Mary wiped at her tears as she recalled the woman's words and the anger she'd heard in them. She shuddered, regretting more than ever that stupid letter she'd written. The heat of humiliation and mortification burned her cheeks. If only she hadn't poured her heart out to him. If only she had just written him about the package and left it at that. If only...

Unfortunately, she'd been feeling nostalgic the night she wrote that letter. Her mare was about to give birth so she was staying the night at the ranch in her old room. She'd come in from the barn late that night, and had seen the package she'd promised to let Chase know about. Not far into the letter, she'd become sad and regretful. Filled with memories of the two of them growing up together on the ranch from the age of fifteen, she'd decide to call him only to find that his number was no longer in service. Then she'd tried to find him on social media. No luck. It was as if he'd dropped off the face of the earth. Had something happened to him?

Worried, she'd gone online and found an address for him but no phone number. In retrospect, she should never have written the letter—not in the mood she'd been in. What she hated most since he hadn't answered her letter or called, was that she had written how much she missed him and how she'd never gotten over him and how she regretted their breakup.

She'd stuffed the letter into the envelope addressed to him and, wiping her tears, had left it on her desk in her old room at the ranch as she climbed into bed. The next morning before daylight her mother had called up to her room to say that the mare had gone into labor. Forgetting all about the letter, she'd been so excited about the new foal that she'd put everything else out of her mind. By the time she remembered the letter, it was gone. Her aunt Stacy had seen it, put a stamp on the envelope and mailed it for her.

At first, Mary had been in a panic, expecting Chase to call as soon as he received the letter. She'd played the conversation in her head every way she thought possible, all but one of them humiliating. As days passed, she'd still held out hope. Now after more than two weeks and that horrible phone call, she knew it was really over and she had to accept it.

Still her heart ached. Chase had been her first love. Did anyone ever get over their first love? He had obviously moved on. Mary took another deep breath and tried to put it out of her mind. She loved summer here in the canyon. The temperature was perfect—never too cold or too hot. A warm breeze swayed the pine boughs and keeled over the tall grass in the pasture nearby. Closer a horse whinnied from the corral next to the barn as a hawk made a slow lazy circle in the clear blue overhead.

Days like this she couldn't imagine living anywhere else. She took another deep breath. She needed to get back to her office. She had work to do. Along with doing the ranch books for Cardwell Ranch, she had taken on work from other ranches in the canyon and built a lucrative business.

She would get over Chase or die trying, she told herself. As she straightened her back, her tears dried, and she walked toward her SUV. She'd give Deputy Dillon Ramsey a call. It was time she moved on. Like falling off a horse, she was ready to saddle up again. Forgetting Chase wouldn't be easy, but if anyone could help the process, she figured Dillon Ramsey was the man to do it.

Chapter Three

Chase was carrying the last of his things out to his pickup when he saw Fiona drive up. He swore under his breath. He'd hoped to leave without a scene. Actually, he'd been surprised that she hadn't come by sooner. As she was friends with Rick's wife, Patty, Chase was pretty sure she had intel into how the packing and leaving had been going.

He braced himself as he walked to his pickup and put the final box into the back. He heard Fiona get out of her car and walk toward him. He figured it could go several ways. She would try seduction or tears or raging fury, or a combination of all three.

Hands deep in the pockets of her jacket as she approached, she gave him a shy smile. It was that smile that had appealed to him that first night. He'd been vulnerable, and he suspected she'd known it. Did she think that smile would work again?

He felt guilty for even thinking that she was so calculating and yet he'd seen the way she'd worked him. "Fiona, I don't want any trouble."

"Trouble?" She chuckled. "I heard you were moving out today. I only wanted to come say goodbye."

Chase wished that was the extent of it, but he'd come to know her better than that. "I think we covered goodbye the last time we saw each other."

She ignored that. "I know you're still angry with me—"

"Fiona—"

Tears welled in her green eyes as if she could call them up at a moment's notice. "Chase, at least give me a hug goodbye. Please." Before he could move, she closed the distance between them. As she did, her hands came out of her jacket pockets. The blade of the knife in her right hand caught the light as she started to put her arms around his neck.

As he jerked back, he grabbed her wrist. "What the—" He cursed as he tightened his grip on her wrist holding the knife. She was stronger than she looked. She struggled to stab him as she screamed obscenities at him.

The look in her eyes was almost more frightening than the knife clutched in her fist. He twisted her wrist until she cried out and dropped the weapon. The moment it hit the ground, he let go of her, realizing he was hurting her.

She dived for the knife, but he kicked it away, chasing after it before she could pick it up again. She leaped at him, pounding on his back as she tried to drag him to the ground.

He threw her off. She stumbled and fell to the grass and began to cry hysterically. He stared down at her. Had she really tried to kill him?

"Don't! Don't kill me!" she screamed, raising her hands as if she thought he was going to stab her. He'd forgotten that he'd picked up the knife, but he wasn't threatening her with it.

He didn't understand what was going on until he realized they were no longer alone. Fiona had an audience. Some of the apartment tenants had come out. One of them, an elderly woman, was fumbling with her phone as if to call the cops.

"Everything is all right," he quickly told the woman.

The older woman looked from Fiona to him and back. Her gaze caught on the knife he was holding at his side.

"There is no reason to call the police," Chase said calmly as he walked to the trash cans lined up along the street, opened one and dropped the knife into the bottom.

"That's my best knife!" Fiona yelled. "You owe me for that."

He saw that the tenant was now staring at Fiona, who was brushing off her jeans as she got to her feet.

"What are you staring at, you old crone? Go back inside before I take that phone away from you and stick it up your—"

"Fiona," Chase said as the woman hurriedly turned and rushed back inside. He shook his head as he gave Fiona a wide berth as he headed toward his apartment to lock up. "Go home before the police come."

"She won't call. She knows I'll come back here if she does."

He hoped Fiona was right about the woman not making the call. Otherwise, he'd be held up making a statement to the police—that's if he didn't end up behind bars. He didn't doubt that Fiona would lie through her teeth about the incident.

"She won't make you happy," Fiona screamed after him as he opened the door to his apartment, keeping an eye on her the whole time. The last thing he wanted was her getting inside. If she didn't have another weapon, he had no doubt she'd find one.

Stopping in the doorway, he looked back at her. Her makeup had run along with her nose. She hadn't bothered to wipe either. She looked small, and for a moment his heart went out to her. What had happened to that professional, together woman he'd met at the party?

"You need to get help, Fi."

She scoffed at that. "You're the one who needs help, Chase."

He stepped inside, closed and locked the door, before sliding the dead bolt. Who's to say she didn't have a half dozen spare keys made. She'd lied about the building manager opening the door for her. She'd lied about a lot of things. He had no idea who Fiona Barkley was. But soon she would be nothing more than a bad memory, he told himself as he finished checking to make sure he hadn't left anything. When he looked out, he saw her drive away.

Only then did he pick up his duffel bag, lock the apartment door behind him and head for his truck, anxious to get on the road to Montana. But as he neared his pickup, he saw what Fiona had left him. On the driver's-side window scrawled crudely in lipstick were the words *You'll regret it.*

That was certainly true. He regretted it already. He wondered what would happen to her and feared for the next man who caught her eye. Maybe the next man would handle it better, he told himself.

Tossing his duffel bag onto the passenger seat, he pulled an old rag from under the seat and wiped off what he could of the lipstick. Then, climbing into this truck, he pointed it toward Montana and Mary, putting Fiona out of his mind.

THERE WERE DAYS when Dana felt all sixty-two of her years. Often when she looked at her twenty-eight-year-old daughter, Mary, she wondered where the years had gone. She felt as if she'd merely blinked and her baby girl had grown into a woman.

Being her first and only daughter, Mary had a special place in her heart. So when Mary hurt, Dana did too. Ever since Chase and Mary had broken up and he'd left town, her daughter had been heartsick, and Dana had had no idea how to help her.

She knew that kind of pain. Hud had broken her heart years ago when they'd disagreed and he'd taken off. But he'd come back, and their love had overcome all the obstacles that had been thrown at them since. She'd hoped that Mary throwing herself into her accounting business would help. But as successful as Mary now was with her business, the building she'd bought, the apartments she'd remodeled and rented, there was a hole in her life—and her heart. A mother could see it.

"Sis, have you heard a word I've said?"

Dana looked from the window where she'd been

watching Mary unsaddling her horse to where her brother sat at the kitchen table across from her. "Sorry. Did you just say *cattle thieves*?"

Jordan shook his head at her and smiled. There'd been a time when she and her brother had been at odds over the ranch. Fortunately, those days were long behind them. He'd often said that the smartest thing he'd ever done was to come back here, make peace and help Dana run Cardwell Ranch. She couldn't agree more.

"We lost another three head. Hud blames paleo diets," Jordan said, and picked up one of the chocolate chip cookies Dana had baked that morning.

"How many does this make?" she asked.

"There's at least a dozen gone," her brother said.

She looked to her husband who sat at the head of the table and had also been watching Mary out the window. Hud reached for another cookie. He came home every day for lunch and had for years. Today she'd made sandwiches and baked his favorite cookies.

"They're hitting at night, opening a gate, cutting out only a few at a time and herding them to the road where they have a truck waiting," the marshal said. "They never hit in the same part of any ranch twice, so unless we can predict where they're going to show up next… We aren't the only ones who've had losses."

"We could hire men to ride the fences at night," Jordan said.

"I'll put a deputy or two on the back roads for a couple of nights and see what we come up with,"

Hud said and, pushing away his plate and getting to his feet, shot Dana a questioning look.

Jordan, apparently recognizing the gesture, also got to his feet and excused himself. As he left, Hud said, "I know something is bothering you, and it isn't rustlers."

She smiled up at him. He knew her so well, her lover, her husband, her best friend. "It's Mary. Stacy told me earlier that she mailed a letter from Mary to Chase a few weeks ago. Mary hasn't heard back."

Hud groaned. "You have any idea what was in the letter?"

"No, but since she's been moping around I'd say she is still obviously in love with him." She shrugged. "I don't think she's ever gotten over him."

Her husband shook his head. "Why didn't we have all boys?"

"Our sons will fall in love one day and will probably have their heartbreaks as well." She had the feeling that Hud hadn't heard the latest. "She's going out with Deputy Dillon Ramsey tonight."

Hud swore and raked a hand through his graying hair. "I shouldn't have mentioned that there was something about him that made me nervous."

She laughed. "If you're that worried about him, then why don't you talk to her?"

Her husband shot her a look that said he knew their stubborn daughter only too well. "Tell her not to do something and damned if she isn't even more bound and determined to do it."

Like he had to tell her that. Mary was just like

her mother and grandmother. "It's just a date," Dana said, hoping there wasn't anything to worry about.

Hud grumbled under his breath as he reached for his Stetson. "I have to get back to work." His look softened. "You think she's all right?"

Dana wished she knew. "She will be, given time. I think she needs to get some closure from Chase. His not answering her letter could be what she needed to move on."

"I hope not with Dillon Ramsey."

"Seriously, what is it about him that worries you?" Dana asked.

He frowned. "I can't put my finger on it. I hired him as a favor to his uncle down in Wyoming. Dillon's cocky and opinionated."

Dana laughed. "I used to know a deputy like that."

Hud grinned. "Point taken. He's also still green."

"I don't think that's the part that caught Mary's attention."

Her husband groaned. "I'd like to see her with someone with both feet firmly planted on the ground."

"You mean someone who isn't in law enforcement. Chase Steele wasn't."

"I liked him well enough," Hud said grudgingly. "But he hadn't sowed his wild oats yet. They were both too young, and he needed to get out of here and get some maturity under his belt, so to speak."

"She wanted him to stay and fight for her. Sound familiar?"

Hud's smile was sad. "Sometimes a man has to go out into the world, grow up, figure some things out." He reached for her hand. "That's what I did when I left. It made me realize what I wanted. You."

She stepped into his arms, leaning into his strength, thankful for the years they'd had together raising a family on this ranch. "Mary's strong."

"Like her mother."

"She'll be all right," Dana said, hoping it was true.

CHASE WAS DETERMINED to drive as far as he could the first day, needing to put miles behind him. He thought of Fiona and felt sick to his stomach. He kept going over it in his head, trying to understand if he'd done anything to lead her on beyond that one night. He was clear with her that he was not in the market for anything serious. His biggest mistake though was allowing himself a moment of weakness when he'd let himself be seduced.

But before that he'd explained to her that he was in love with someone else. She said she didn't care. That she wasn't looking for a relationship. She'd said that she needed him that night because she'd had a bad day.

Had he really fallen for that? He had. And when she became obsessed, he'd been shocked and felt sorry for her. Maybe he shouldn't have.

He felt awful, and not even the miles he put behind him made him feel better. He wished he'd never left Montana, but at the time, leaving seemed the only thing to do. He'd worked his way south, taking carpenter jobs, having no idea where he was headed.

When he'd gotten the call from his mother to say she was dying and that she'd needed to see him, he'd quit his job, packed up and headed for Quartsite, Arizona, in hopes that his mother would finally give him the name.

Chase had never known who his father was. It was a secret his mother refused to reveal for reasons of her own. Once in Arizona, though, he'd realized that she planned to take that secret to her grave. On her death bed, she'd begged him to do one thing for her. Would he take her ashes back to Montana and scatter them in the Gallatin Canyon near Big Sky?

"That's where I met your father," she said, her voice weak. "He was the love of my life."

She hadn't given him a name, but at least he knew now that the man had lived in Big Sky at the time of Chase's conception. It wasn't much, but it was better than nothing.

HE WAS IN the middle of nowhere just outside of Searchlight, Nevada, when smoke began to boil out from under the pickup's hood. He started to pull over when the engine made a loud sound and stopped dead. As he rolled to stop, his first thought was: could Fiona have done something to his pickup before he left?

Anger filled him to overflowing. But it was another emotion that scared him. He had a sudden awful feeling that something terrible was going to happen to Mary if he didn't get to Montana. Soon. The feeling was so strong that he thought about leaving his pickup beside the road and thumbing a ride the rest of the way.

Chase tried to tamp down the feeling, telling himself that it was because of Fiona and what she'd done before he'd left when she'd tried to kill him, not to mention what she'd done to his pickup. The engine was shot. He'd have to get a new one and that was going to take a while.

That bad feeling though wouldn't go away. After he called for a tow truck, he dialed the Jensen Ranch, the closest ranch to Mary's. He figured if anyone would know how Mary was doing, it would be Beth Anne Jensen. She answered on the third ring. "It's Chase." He heard the immediate change in her voice and realized she was probably the wrong person to call, but it was too late. Beth Anne had liked him a little too much when he'd worked for her family and it had caused a problem between him and Mary.

"Hey Chase. Are you back in town?"

"No, I was just calling to check on Mary. I was worried about her. I figured you'd know how she's doing. Is everything all right with her?"

Beth Anne's tone changed from sugar to vinegar. "As far as I know everything is just great with her. Is that all you wanted to know?"

This was definitely a mistake. "How are you?"

"I opened my own flower shop. I've been dating a rodeo cowboy. I'm just fine, as if you care." She sighed. "So if you're still hung up on Mary, why haven't you come back?"

Stubbornness. Stupidity. Pride. A combination of all three. "I just had a sudden bad feeling that she might be in trouble."

Beth Anne laughed. "Could be, now that you mention it. My brother saw her earlier out with some young deputy. Apparently, she's dating him."

"Sounds like she's doing fine then. Thanks. You take care." He swore as he disconnected and put his worry about Mary out of his mind. She should be plenty safe dating a deputy, right? He gave his front tire a kick, then paced as he waited for the tow truck.

It HAD TAKEN hours before the tow truck had arrived. By then the auto shop was closed. He'd registered at a motel, taken a hot shower and sprawled on the bed, furious with Fiona, but even more so with himself.

He'd known he had a serious problem when he'd seen the smoke roiling out from under the hood. When the engine seized up, he'd known it was blown before he'd climbed out and lifted the hood.

At first, he couldn't understand what had happened. The pickup wasn't brand-new, but it had been in good shape. The first thing he'd checked was the oil. That's when he'd smelled it. Bleach.

The realization had come in a flash. He'd thrown a container of bleach away in his garbage just that morning, along with some other household cleaners that he didn't want to carry all the way back to Montana. He'd seen the bleach bottle when he'd tossed Fiona's knife into one of the trash cans at the curb.

Now, lying on the bed in the motel, Chase swore. He'd left Fiona out there alone with his pickup. He'd thought the only mischief she'd gotten up to was writing on his pickup window with lipstick. He'd underestimated her, and now it was going to cost him dearly.

He'd have to have a new engine put in the truck, and that was going to take both money and time.

THREE DAYS LATER, while waiting in Henderson, Nevada for his new engine to be installed, he called Rick.

"Hey, Chase, great to hear from you. How far did you make it? I thought you might have decided to drive straight through all night."

"I broke down near Searchlight."

"Really? Is it serious?"

"I'm afraid so. The engine blew. I suspect Fiona put bleach in the oil."

Rick let out a curse. "That would seize up the engine."

"That's exactly what it did."

"Oh, man I am so sorry. Listen, I am beginning to feel like this is all my fault. Is there anything I can do? Where are you now? I could drive up there, maybe bring one of the big trailers. We could haul your pickup back down here. I know a mechanic—"

"I appreciate it, but I'm getting it fixed here in Henderson. That's not why I called."

"It's funny you should call," Rick said. "I was about to call you, but I kept putting it off hoping to have better news."

His heart began to pound. "What's wrong?"

His former boss let out a dry chuckle. "We're still friends, right?"

"Right. I forgave you for Fiona if that's what you're worried about."

"You might change your mind after you hear what

I have to tell you," Rick said. "I didn't want you to hear this on the news." He felt his stomach drop as he waited for the bad news. "Fiona apparently hasn't been at work since before you left. Patty went over to her place. Her car was gone and there was no sign of her. But she'd called Patty the night you left from a bar and was pretty wasted and incoherent. When Patty wasn't able to reach her in the days that followed, she finally went over to her condo. It appeared she hadn't been back for a few days." Chase swore. She wouldn't hurt herself, would she? She'd said he would regret it. He felt a sliver of fear race up his spine. As delusional as the woman was—

Rick cleared his voice. "This morning a fisherman found her car in the Colorado River."

His breath caught in his throat. "Is she…?"

"They're dragging the river for her body, but it's hard to say how far her body might have gone downstream. The river was running pretty high after the big thunderstorm they had up in the mountains a few days ago."

Chase raked a hand through his hair as he paced the floor of his motel room as he'd been doing for days now. "She threatened to do all kinds of things, but I never thought she'd do something like this."

"Before you jump to conclusions, the police think it could have been an accident. Fiona was caught on video leaving the club that night and appeared to be quite inebriated," Rick said. "Look, this isn't your fault. I debated even telling you. Fiona was irrational. My wife said she's feared that the woman's been headed for a violent end for a long time, you know?"

He nodded to himself as he stopped to look out the motel room window at the heat waves rising off desert floor and yearned for Montana. "Still I hate to think she might have done this on purpose because of me."

"She wasn't right in the head. Anyway, it was probably an accident. I'm sorry to call with this kind of news, but I thought you'd want to know. Once your pickup's fixed you'll be heading out and putting all of this behind you. Still thinking about going to Colorado? You know I'd love to have you back."

No reason not to tell him now. "I'm headed home as soon as the pickup's fixed, but thanks again for the offer."

"Home to Montana? You really never got over this woman, huh."

"No, I never did." He realized that when he thought of home, it was Mary he thought of. Her and the Gallatin Canyon. "It's where I grew up. Where I first fell in love."

"Well, I wish you luck. I hope it goes well."

"Thanks. If you hear anything else about Fiona—"

"I'll keep it to myself."

"No, call me. I really didn't know the woman. But I care about what happened to her." He thought of the first night he'd seen her, all dressed up in that dark suit and looking so strong and capable. And the other times when she'd stopped by his apartment looking as if she'd just come home from spring break and acting the part. "It was like she was always changing before my eyes. I never knew who she was. I'm not sure she did."

He and Rick said goodbye again. Disconnecting, he pocketed his phone. He couldn't help wondering about Fiona's last moments underwater inside her car. Did she know how to swim? He had no idea. Was it too deep for her to reach the surface? Or had she been swept away?

Chase felt sad, but he knew there was no way he could have helped her. She wanted a man committed to her, and she deserved it. But as he'd told her that first night, he wasn't that man.

If only he had known how broken and damaged she was. He would have given her a wide berth. He should have anyway, and now he blamed himself for his moment of weakness. That night he'd needed someone, but that someone had been Mary, not a woman he didn't know. Not Fiona.

"I'm so sorry," he whispered. "I'm so sorry." He hoped that maybe now Fiona would finally be at peace.

Looking toward the wide-open horizon, he turned his thoughts to Mary. He couldn't wait to look into her beautiful blue eyes and tell her that he'd never stopped loving her. That thought made him even more anxious. He couldn't wait to get home.

DILLON WALKED HER to her door and waited while Mary pulled out her keys.

"I had a wonderful time," he said as he leaned casually against the side of her building as if waiting to see if she was going to invite him up. Clouds scudded past the full moon to disappear over the mountaintops surrounding the canyon. The cool night air smelled of pine and clear blue trout stream water. This part of Montana was a little bit of Heaven, her mother was fond of saying. Mary agreed.

She'd left a light on in her apartment on the top floor. It glowed a warm inviting golden hue.

"I had fun too," she said, and considered asking him up to see the view from what she jokingly called her penthouse. The balcony off the back would be especially nice tonight. But her tongue seemed tied, and suddenly she felt tired and close to tears.

"I should go," Dillon said, his gaze locking with hers. He seemed about to take a step back, but changed his mind and leaned toward her. His hand cupped her jaw as he kissed her. Chastely at first, then with more ardor, gently drawing her to him. The kiss took her by surprise. Their first date he hadn't even tried.

His tongue probed her mouth for a moment before he ended the kiss as abruptly as it had begun. Stepping back, he seemed to study her in the moonlight for a moment before he said, "I really do have to go. Maybe we could do something this weekend if you aren't busy?"

She nodded dumbly. She and Dillon were close to the same age, both adults. She'd expected him to kiss her on their first date. So her surprise tonight had nothing to do with him kissing her, she thought as she entered her building, locking the door behind her and hurrying up to her apartment.

It had everything to do with the kiss.

Mary unlocked her apartment door with trembling fingers, stepped in and locked it behind her.

She leaned against the door, hot tears filling her eyes as she told herself she shouldn't be disappointed. But she was.

The kiss had been fine, as far as kisses went. But even when Dillon had deepened the kiss, she had felt nothing but emptiness. The memory made her feel sick. Would she always compare every kiss with Chase's? Would every man she met come up lacking?

She didn't bother to turn on a lamp as she tossed her purse down and headed toward her bedroom, furious with herself. And even more furious with Chase. He'd left her and Montana as if what they had together meant nothing to him. Clearly it didn't. That's why he'd gotten engaged and wasn't man enough to call her himself and tell her.

Still mentally kicking herself for writing that letter to him, she changed into her favorite T-shirt and went into the bathroom to brush her teeth. Her image in the mirror startled her. She was no longer that young girl that Chase had fallen in love with. She was a woman in her own right. She dried her tears, the crying replaced with angry determination. If that was the way Chase wanted to be, then it was fine with her.

Her cell phone rang, startling her. She hurried to it, and for just a moment she thought it was going to be Chase. Her heart had soared, then come crashing down. Chase had moved on. When was she going to accept that?

"I couldn't quit thinking about you after I left," Dillon said. "I was wondering if you'd like to go to the movies tomorrow night?"

She didn't hesitate. "I'd love to." Maybe she just hadn't been ready for his kiss. Maybe next time...

"Great," Dillon said. "I'll pick you up at 5:30 if that's all right. We can grab something to eat before we go to the theater."

"Sounds perfect." If Chase could see her now, she thought as she hung up. Dillon was handsome, but less rugged looking than Chase. Taller though by a good inch or two, and he wanted to go out with her.

She disconnected, determined to put Chase Steele behind her. He had moved on and now she was too. Next time, she would invite Dillon up to her apartment. But even as she thought it, she imagined Chase and the woman he was engaged to. While she was busy comparing every man she met to him, he'd found someone and fallen in love. It made her question if what she and Chase once had was really that unique and special. Just because it had been for her...

Mary willed herself not to think about him. She touched her tongue to her lower lip. Dillon had made her laugh, and he'd certainly been attentive. While the kiss hadn't spurred a reaction in her, she was willing to give it another chance.

Her father didn't trust the man, so didn't that mean that there was more to Dillon than met the eye? Chase had always been a little wild growing up. Her father had been worried about her relationship with him. Maybe there was some wildness in Dillon that would make him more interesting.

As she fell asleep though, her thoughts returned to Chase until her heart was aching and tears were leaking onto her pillow.

Chapter Four

"How was your date?"

Mary looked up the next morning to find her mother standing in the doorway of her office holding two cups of coffee from the shop across the street. "Tell me that's an ultimate caramel frappaccino."

Dana laughed. "Do you mean layers of whipped cream infused with rich coffee, white chocolate and dark caramel? Each layer sitting on a dollop of dark caramel sauce?"

"Apparently I've mentioned why I love it," she said, smiling at her mother as Dana handed her the cup. She breathed in the sweet scent for a moment before she licked some of the whipped cream off the top. "I hope you got one of these for yourself."

"Not likely," her mother said as she sat down across the desk from her. "The calories alone scared me off. Anyway, you know I prefer my coffee to actually taste like coffee. That's why I drink it black."

Mary grimaced and shook her head, always amazed how much she looked like her mother but the similarities seemed to have stopped there. What they shared was their love of Montana and determi-

nation to keep Cardwell Ranch for future genera-
tions. At least for the ones who wanted to stay here.
Her three brothers had left quickly enough, thrown
to the far winds. She wondered about her own children—when she had them one day with the man she
eventually married. Would they feel wanderlust like
Chase had? She knew she wouldn't be able to make
them stay nearby any more than she had him.

She took a sip of her coffee, hating that she'd let
her thoughts wander down that particular path.

"I'm trying to tell if the date went well or not," her
mother said, studying her openly. "When I walked
in, I thought it had, but now you're frowning. Is your
coffee all right?"

Mary replaced her frown with a smile as she
turned her attention to her mother and away from
Chase. "My coffee is amazing. Thank you so much.
It was just what I needed. Normally I try to get over
to Lone Peak Perk when it opens, but this morning
I was anxious to get to work. I wish they delivered."

Her mother gave her a pointed look. "Are you purposely avoiding talking about your date, because I'm
more interested in it than your coffee habit."

Laughing, she said, "The date was fine. Good.
Fun, actually. We're going out again tonight."

Her mother raised a brow. "Again already? So
he was a perfect gentleman?" Her mother took a sip
of her coffee as if pretending she wasn't stepping
over a line.

"You're welcome to tell Dad that he was," she said
with a twinkle in her eye.

"Mary!" They both laughed. "So you like him?"

Mary nodded. *Like* was exactly the right word. She had hoped to feel more.

"You are impossible. You're determined to make me drag everything out of you, aren't you?"

"Not everything," she said coyly. Her mother seemed to like this game they played. Mostly Dana seemed relieved that Mary was moving on after Chase. She didn't like to see her daughter unhappy, Mary thought. It was time to quit moping over Chase, and they both knew it.

"So how did we do?" Deputy Dillon Ramsey asked his friend as he closed the cabin door and headed for the refrigerator for a beer as if he lived there.

"Picked up another three head of prime beef," Grady Birch said, and quickly added, "They were patrolling the fences last night just like you said they would be. Smart to hit a ranch on the other side of the river. We got in and out. No sweat."

"It's nice that I know where the deputies will be watching." Dillon grinned as he popped the top on his beer can and took a long swig.

"Trouble is, I heard around town that ranchers are going to start riding their fences. Word's out."

Dillon swore. "It was such easy pickings for a while." He plopped down in one of the worn chairs in Grady's cabin, feeling more at home in this ratty-ass place than in his nice apartment in Big Sky. "So we'll cool it until the heat dies down."

"Back to easy pickings, how did your date go?"

He grinned. "A couple more dates and I'll have her eating out of my hand."

Grady looked worried. "You're playing with fire, you know. The marshal's daughter?" His friend shook his head. "You sure this game you're playing is worth it?"

Dillon laughed. "To be able to drive out to the Cardwell Ranch, sit on that big porch of theirs and drink the marshal's beer right under his nose? You damn betcha it's worth it."

"Maybe I don't understand the end game," Grady suggested.

"I need this job until I can get enough money together to go somewhere warm, sit in the shade and drink fancy drinks with umbrellas in them for the rest of my life. I have plans for my future and they don't include a woman, especially Mary Savage. But in the meantime…" He smiled and took a slug of his beer. "She ain't half bad to look at. For her age, I get the feeling that she hasn't had much experience. I'd be happy to teach her a few things."

"Well, it still seems dangerous dating his daughter," Grady said. "Unless you're not telling me the truth and you're serious about her."

"I'm only serious about keeping the marshal from being suspicious of me. I told you, he almost caught me that one night after we hit the Cardwell Ranch. I had to do some fast talking, but I think I convinced him that I was patrolling the area on my night off."

"And dating his daughter will make him less suspicious of you?"

"It will give him something else to worry about," Dillon said with a grin. He knew he'd gotten the job only because of his uncle. He'd gone into law enforcement at his uncle's encouragement. Also, he'd seen it as a get-out-of-jail-free card. No one would suspect a cop, right?

Unfortunately, his uncle had been more than suspicious about what Dillon had been doing to make some extra money. So it had come down to him leaving Wyoming to take the deputy job in the Gallatin Canyon of Montana.

"Mary Savage is a good-looking woman, no doubt about that," Grady said as he got up to get them more beer.

Dillon watched him with narrowed eyes. "Don't get any ideas. I've been priming this pump for a while now. And believe me, with your record, you wouldn't want Marshal Hud Savage looking too closely at *you*. That's one reason we can't be seen together. As far as anyone knows, you and I aren't even friends."

MARSHAL HUD SAVAGE had been waiting patiently for the call since Deputy Dillon Ramsey had gone off duty. Still, when his phone rang, it made him jump. It wasn't like him to be nervous. Then again, this was about his daughter. He had every right given his feelings about Dillon Ramsey.

He picked up the phone, glad to hear the voice of Hayes Cardwell, Dana's cousin, on the other end of the line. It was nice to have several private investigators in the family. "Well?"

"You were right. He headed out of town the moment he changed out of his uniform," Hayes said. "He went to a cabin back in the hills outside Gallatin

Gateway. You're probably more interested in who is renting the cabin than who owns it. Ever heard of a man named Grady Birch?"

The name didn't ring any bells. "Who is he?"

"He has an interesting rap sheet that includes theft and assault. He's done his share of cattle rustling."

"And Dillon went straight there."

"He did. In fact, he's still inside. I'm watching the place from down the road with binoculars."

"So it's away from other houses," Hud said. "Any chance there's a truck around with a large horse trailer?"

"The kind that could be used to steal cattle?"

"Exactly," the marshal said.

"There's an old one parked out back. If they both leave, I might get a chance to have a look inside."

"I doubt they're going to leave together," Hud said. "Thanks for doing this but I can take it from here."

"No problem. What's family for?"

"I'll expect a bill for your time," the marshal said. "Or I'll tell Dana on you."

Hayes laughed. "Don't want *her* mad at me."

"No one does. Also," Hud added, "let's keep this just between the two of us for now." He disconnected and called up Grady Birch's rap sheet. Hayes was right. Grady was trouble. So why wasn't he surprised that his new deputy was hanging out with a man like that?

He'd known it the moment he laid eyes on the handsome lawman. Actually, he'd suspected there would be a problem when Dillon's uncle called, asking for the favor. He'd wanted to turn the man down, but the uncle was a good cop who Hud had worked with on a case down in Jackson, Wyoming.

Hud rubbed a hand over his face. Dillon was everything he'd suspected he was, and now he was dating Mary. He swore. What was he going to do about it? In the first place, he had no proof. Yet. So warning Mary about him would be a waste of breath even if she *didn't* find something romantic about dating an outlaw. Some people still saw cattle rustling as part of an Old West tradition. Also, his daughter was too old to demand that she stop seeing Dillon.

No, he was going to have to handle this very delicately, and delicate wasn't in his repertoire. That didn't leave him many options. Catching Dillon redhanded wouldn't be easy because the deputy wasn't stupid. Arresting him without enough evidence to put him away was also a bad move.

Hud knew he had to bide his time. He told himself that maybe he'd get lucky, and Dillon or Grady would make a mistake. He just hoped it was soon, before Mary got any more involved with the man.

CHASE FINALLY GOT the call. His pickup engine was in and he could come by this afternoon to pick it up. He hadn't talked to Rick in a few days and feeling at loose ends, pulled out his cell phone and made the call, dreading the news. Rick answered on the second ring.

"Has there been any word on Fiona?" The silence on the other end of the line stretched out long enough that Chase knew what was coming.

"They gave up the search. The general consensus is that her body washed downstream and will be found once the water goes down more."

"I'm sorry to hear that. I'm sure Patty is upset."

"She is," Rick said. "She felt sorry for Fiona. That's why she didn't cut ties with her after high school. Patty's over at Fiona's condo now cleaning it out since she has no next of kin. She found out from a bank statement that Fiona had drained her bank account almost a week ago. Took all of it in cash. Who knows what she did with that much money. Hell, it could be in the river with her. Patty's going to try to organize some kind of service for her."

"She doesn't have any family?"

"I guess I didn't tell you. Her whole family died in a fire when Fiona was eleven. She would have perished with her parents and three older stepbrothers, but she'd stayed over at a friend's house that night."

"Oh man. That could explain a lot," he said more to himself. "I wish I'd known all of this. Maybe I could have handled things better."

"Trust me, it would take a psychiatrist years to sort that woman out. So stop blaming yourself. I'm the one who should have warned you. But it's over now."

The fact that he felt relieved made him feel even more guilty as he promised to stay in touch and hung up.

Chapter Five

"Just fill out this application and leave it," the barista said as she dropped the form on the table in front of the dark-haired woman with the pixie haircut and the kind of cute Southern accent and lisp because of the gap between her front teeth.

She'd introduced herself as Lucy Carson, as if Christy was supposed to recognize the name.

"You're sure there's no chance of an opening soon?" Lucy Carson asked now before glancing at her name tag and adding, "Christy."

Christy shook her head. "Like I said. I just got hired, so I really doubt there will be anything for the rest of the season unless someone quits and that's unlikely. Jobs aren't that easy to find in Big Sky. Your application will be on file with dozens of others, so if I were you, I'd keep looking."

She didn't mean to sound cruel or dismissive, but she'd told the woman there weren't any openings. Still, the woman had insisted on filling out an application. If she wanted to waste her time, then Christy wasn't going to stop her. She just thought it was stupid.

From behind the counter, she watched how neatly Lucy Carson filled in each blank space. Was it stubbornness or arrogance? The lady acted as if she thought the manager would let someone go to hire *her*. That sounded like arrogance to Christy.

"What about a place to live nearby?" the woman asked, looking up from the application.

Christy laughed. "You'll have even worse luck finding an apartment. I've been waiting for months to get into the one across the street, and it's just a small bedroom."

Lucy glanced in the direction she pointed. "There's rentals over there?"

"There *was*. I got the last one. I'm moving in tomorrow." This Lucy was starting to get on her nerves. She found herself wishing that some customers would come in just so she had something to do. Usually she loved the slow afternoons when she could look at magazines and do absolutely nothing, even though she was supposed to be cleaning on her downtime.

The woman studied her for a moment, then smiled and resumed filling out the application.

"You should go down to Bozeman," Christy told her. "More opportunities in a college town than here in the canyon." Jobs weren't easy to get in Big Sky especially during the busy times, summer, and winter. Not just that, this job didn't even pay that well. Too many young people would work for nothing just to get to spend their free time up on the mountain biking and kayaking in the summer, skiing and snowboarding in the winter.

The woman finished and brought her application over to the counter. Christy glanced at the name. "Is Lucy short for something?" she asked.

"My mother was a huge fan of *I Love Lucy* reruns."

She looked at the application, almost feeling sorry for the young woman. According to this, she had a lot of experience as a barista but then so did a whole lot of other people. "I see you didn't put down an address." She looked up at the woman who gave her a bright smile.

"Remember, I'm still looking for a place to stay, but once I start working I'm sure an apartment will open up."

Christy couldn't help but chuckle under her breath at the woman's naive optimism. "Most everyone who works in Big Sky ends up commuting at least forty miles a day. There just aren't any cheap rentals for minimum wage workers even if you should luck out and get a job."

Lucy smiled. "I'm not worried. Things just tend to work out for me. I'm lucky that way."

Whatever, Christy thought. "I'll give your application to Andrea but like I said, we don't have any openings."

"Not yet anyway," Lucy said. "So where do you go to have fun on a Saturday night?"

"Charley's if you like country. Otherwise—"

"I'm betting you like country music," Lucy said. "Your car with the George Strait bumper sticker gives you away."

"My car?" Christy frowned.

"Isn't that your SUV parked across the street?"

She looked out the window and laughed. "Not hardly. Mine is that little blue beat-up sedan with all the stuff in the back since I can't move into my apartment until tomorrow. I've been waiting for weeks, staying with my mother down in Bozeman and driving back and forth when I can't find someone to stay with here. Do you have any family you could stay with?"

Lucy shook her head. "No family. Just me. Maybe I'll check out Charley's tonight." She smiled her gaptoothed smile. "Hopefully I'll get lucky and some handsome cowboy will take me home with him. Or maybe it's not that kind of place."

"No, it is. There'll be cowboys and ski bums."

"I might see you there then?" Lucy said. "Don't worry. I won't intrude if you've found your own cowboy. I'm guessing there's one you're planning to meet tonight."

Christy felt herself flush. "Not exactly. I'm just hoping he'll be there."

Lucy laughed. "Hoping to get lucky, huh? Well, thanks again for your help." She left smiling, making Christy shake her head as she tossed Lucy's application on the desk in Andrea's office. She'd ended up almost liking the woman. Now if she could just get through the rest of the day. She was excited about tonight at Charley's. She did feel lucky. She had a job, an apartment to move into tomorrow and with even more luck, she would be going home with the man she had a crush on. Otherwise, she would be sleeping in her car on top of all her belongings.

Tomorrow though, she'd be moving into the apartment across the street that Mary Savage owned. How handy was that since she could sleep late and still get to work on time with her job just across the street?

LUCY CARSON WAS also looking at the small apartment house across the street from Lone Peak Perk as she walked to her car. She had her heart set on a job at the coffee shop and an apartment across the street in Mary Cardwell Savage's building. Not that she always got what she set her heart on, she thought bitterly, but she would make this happen, whatever she had to do.

As she climbed into her new car, she breathed in the scent of soft leather. She really did like the smell of a new car. Her other one was at the bottom of the Colorado River—or at least it had been until a few weeks ago when it was discovered.

Her disappearing act had gone awry when she'd tried to get out of the car and couldn't before it plummeted toward the river that night. By the time she reached the bank way downriver, she'd wished she'd come up with a better plan. She'd almost died and she wanted to live. More than wanted to live. She'd wanted to kill someone. Especially the person responsible for making her have to go to such extremes: Chase Steele. As she'd sat on that riverbank in the dark, she knew exactly what she had to do. Fortunately, when she'd tried to bail out of the car, she'd grabbed her purse. She'd almost forgotten the money. Her plan really would have gone badly if she'd lost all this money. With it, she could do anything she wanted.

But as close a call as it had been, everything had worked out better than even she'd planned. The authorities thought she was dead, her body rotting downriver. Fiona Barkley was dead. She was free of her. Now she could become anyone she chose.

Since then she'd had to make a few changes, including her name. But she'd never liked the name Fiona anyway. She much preferred Lucy Carson. Getting an ID in that name had been easier than she imagined. It had been harder to give up her long blond hair. But the pixie cut, the dark brown contacts and the brunette hair color transformed her into a woman not even she recognized. She thought she looked good—just not so good that Chase would recognize her.

Her resulting car wreck had pretty much taken care of her change in appearance as well. She had unsnapped her seat belt to make her leap from the car before it hit the water. Had she not been drunk and partway out of the car, she wouldn't have smashed her face, broken her nose and knocked out her front teeth.

As it turned out, that too proved to be a stroke of luck. She'd lost weight because it had hurt to eat. When she looked in the mirror now, she felt she was too skinny, but she knew once she was happy again, she'd put some pounds back on. She still had curves. She always had.

It was her face that had changed the most. Her nose had healed but it had a slight lean to it. She

liked the imperfection. Just as she liked the gap between her two new front teeth. It had taken going to
a dentist in Mexico to get a rush job. She liked the
gap. It had even changed the way she talked giving
her a little lisp. She'd been able to pick up her former
Southern accent without any trouble since it was the
way she'd talked before college. It was enough of a
change in her appearance and voice that she knew
she could get away with it—as long as she never got
too close to Chase.

In the meantime, she couldn't wait to meet Mary
Cardwell Savage.

MARY STOOD ACROSS the street from Lone Peak Perk
thinking about her date last night with Dillon. She'd
seen the slim, dark-haired woman come out of the
coffee shop and get into a gray SUV, but her mind
had been elsewhere. As the SUV pulled away, she
turned from the window, angry with herself.

She was still holding out hope that Chase would
contact her. The very thought made her want to shake
herself. It had been weeks. If he was going to answer,
he would have a long time ago. So why did she keep
thinking she'd hear from him? Hadn't his fiancée told
him that she'd called? Maybe he thought that was
sufficient. Not the man she'd known, she thought.

And that was what kept nagging at her. She'd
known Chase since he was fifteen. He'd come to
work for the Jensen Ranch next door. Mary's mom
had pretty much adopted him after finding out the
reason he'd been sent to live in the canyon was because his mother couldn't take care of him. Muriel

was going through cancer treatment. He'd been honorable even at a young age. He wasn't the kind of man not to call and tell her about a fiancée.

So his not calling or writing felt…wrong. And it left her with nagging questions.

That was only part of the problem and she knew it. She'd hoped that Dillon Ramsey would take her mind off Chase. They'd been dating regularly, and most of the time she enjoyed herself. They'd kissed a few times but that was all. He hadn't even made a pass at her. She couldn't imagine what it was about Dillon that had worried her father. At one point, she'd wondered if her father the marshal had warned him to behave with her.

The thought made her cringe. He wouldn't do that, would he?

She'd asked Dillon last night how he liked working for her dad.

"I like it. He's an okay dude," he'd answered.

She'd laughed. No one called her father a dude.

Now, she had to admit that Dillon was a disappointment. Which made her question what it was she was looking for in a man. A sense of adventure along with a sense of humor. Dillon didn't seem to have either.

Was that why she felt so restless? She looked around her apartment, which she'd furnished with things she loved from the turquoise couch to the weathered log end tables and bright flowered rug. But the spectacular view was the best part. The famous Lone Peak, often snowcapped, was framed in her living room window. The mountain looked especially beautiful in the moonlight.

Which made her think of Chase and how much she would have liked to stand on her back deck in the moonlight and kiss him—instead of Dillon. She groaned, remembering her hesitation again last night to invite Dillon up to her apartment. He'd been hinting that he really wanted to see it. She could tell last night that he'd been hurt and a little angry that she hadn't invited him up.

Standing here in the life she'd built, all she could think about was what Chase's opinion would be of it. Would he be proud of her accomplishments? Would he regret ever leaving her?

She shook him from her head and hurried back downstairs. She still had work to do, and all she was doing right now was giving herself a headache.

BY THE NEXT MORNING, news of the hit and run death of Christy Shores had spread through most of Big Sky and the canyon.

As Marshal Hud Savage walked into Charley's, the last place Christy Shores had been seen alive, he saw the bartender from last night wasn't alone.

"Mike French, bartender, right?" Hud asked the younger of the two men standing nervously behind the bar. Twentysomething, Mike looked like a lot of the young people in Big Sky from his athletic build to the T-shirt and shorts over long underwear and sandals.

If Hud had to guess, he'd say Mike had at least one degree in something practical like engineering, but had gotten hooked on a lifestyle of snowboarding in the winter and mountain biking or kayaking in the summer. Which explained the bartending job.

He considered the handsome young man's deep tan from spending more hours outside than bartending. It made him wonder why a man like that had never appealed to his only daughter.

He suspected Mary was too much of a cowgirl to fall for a ski bum. Instead, she was now dating his deputy, Dillon Ramsey. That thought made his stomach roil, considering what he suspected about the man.

The bartender stepped forward to shake his hand. "Bill said you had some questions about Christy?"

Hud nodded and looked to the bar owner, Bill Benson, before he turned back to Mike. "I understand she was one of the last people to leave the bar last night?"

Mike nodded as Hud pulled out his notebook and pen. "I was just about to lock up when she came out of the women's bathroom. She looked like she'd been crying. I hadn't realized she was in there since I had already locked the front door." He shot a guilty look at his boss. "I usually check to make sure everyone was gone, but last night…"

"What was different about last night?" Hud asked.

Mike shifted on his feet. "A fight had broken out earlier between a couple of guys." He shot another look at Bill and added, "Christy had gotten into the middle of it. Not sure what it was about. After I broke it up, I didn't see her. I thought she'd left."

"Christy's blood alcohol was three times the legal limit," Hud said.

Again Mike shot a look at his boss before holding up his hands and quickly defending himself. "I cut her off before the fight because she'd been hitting the booze pretty hard. But that doesn't mean she quit drinking. The place was packed last night. All I know is that I didn't serve her after that."

Hud glanced toward the front door. "Her car is still parked outside. You didn't happen to take her keys, did you?"

The young man grimaced. "I asked for her keys, but she swore to me that she was walking home." He shrugged. "I guess that part was true."

Hud had Christy's car keys in a plastic evidence bag in his patrol SUV. The keys had been found near her body next to the road after she was apparently struck by a vehicle and knocked into the ditch.

"I'm going to need the names of the two men who were involved in the fight," he said. He wrote them down, hiding his surprise when he wrote Grady Birch, but Chet Jensen was no surprise. Chet seemed to think of the local jail as his home away from home. "What about friends, girlfriends, anyone Christy was close to."

Mike shook his head. "She hadn't been working at Lone Peak Perk very long. I'm not sure she'd made any friends yet. When she came into the bar, she was always alone. I think someone said that she was driving back and forth for work from Bozeman where she was living with her mom."

"Did she always leave alone?" he asked.

With a shake of his head, the bartender said, "No." He motioned toward the names he'd given the marshal. "It was usually with one or the other of those two."

Hud thanked Mike and went outside to the car. He'd already run the plates. The vehicle was registered to Christy Shores. Bill came out and drove off, followed by Mike who hopped on his mountain bike.

Christy's older model sedan wasn't locked Hud noted as he pulled on latex gloves and tried the driver's-side door. It swung open with a groan. He looked inside. Neatness apparently wasn't one of the young woman's traits. The back seat was stuffed full of clothing and boxes. He'd been told that she was planning to move into an apartment on the second floor of Mary's building today. The front floorboard on the passenger side was knee-deep in fast-food wrappers and Lone Peak Perk go cups.

He leaned in and took a whiff, picking up the stale scent of cigarettes and alcohol. All his instincts told him that after the apparent night Christy'd had, she would have driven home drunk rather than walk.

On impulse, he slid behind the wheel, inserted the key and turned it. There was only a click. He tried again. Same dull click. Reaching for the hood release, he pulled it and then climbed out to take a look at the engine, suspecting an old battery.

But he was in for a surprise. The battery appeared to be new. The reason the car hadn't started was because someone had purposely disabled it. He could see fresh screwdriver marks on the top of the battery.

Hud suspected that whoever had tampered with

her battery was the same person who had wanted
Christy to take off walking down this road late last
night.

WHEN MARY WALKED across the street to the Lone
Peak Perk the next morning, she was surprised to
find her favorite coffee shop closed. There was a sign
on the door announcing that there'd been a death.

She wondered who had died as she retraced her
footsteps to climb into her pickup and head for the
ranch. Cardwell Ranch was a half mile from Meadow
Village on the opposite side of the Gallatin River.
She always loved this drive because even though
short, the landscape changed so drastically.

Mary left behind housing and business developments, traffic and noise. As she turned off Highway
191 onto the private bridge that crossed the river to
the ranch the roar of the flowing river drowned out
the busy resort town. Towering pines met her on
the other side. She wound back into the mountains
through them before the land opened again for her
first glimpse that day of the ranch buildings.

Behind the huge barn and corrals, the mountains
rose all the way to Montana's Big Sky. She breathed
it all in, always a little awed each time she saw it,
knowing what it took to hang on to a ranch through
hard times. Behind the barn and corrals were a series
of small guest cabins set back against the mountainside. Her aunt Stacy lived in the larger one, the roof
barely visible behind the dark green of the pines.

At the Y in the road, she turned left instead of
continuing back into the mountains to where her

Uncle Jordan and his wife, Liza, lived. The two-story log and stone ranch house where she'd been raised came into view moments later, the brick-red metal roof gleaming in the morning sun.

There were several vehicles parked out front, her father's patrol SUV one of them. When she pushed open the front door, she could hear the roar of voices coming from the kitchen and smiled. This had been the sound she'd come downstairs to every morning for years growing up here.

Mary knew how much her mother loved a full house. It had been hard on her when all of her children had grown up and moved out. But there were still plenty of relatives around. Mary had seven uncles and as many aunts, along with a few cousins who still lived in the area.

As she entered the kitchen, she saw that there was the usual group of family, friends and ranch hands sitting around the huge kitchen table. This morning was no exception. Her uncle Jordan signaled that it was time to get to work, giving her a peck on her cheek as he rose and headed out the door, a half dozen ranch hands following him like baby ducks.

Mary said hello to her aunt Stacy and kissed her mother on the cheek before going to the cupboard to pull down a mug and fill it with coffee. There was always a pot going at Cardwell Ranch. The kitchen had quieted down with Jordan and the ranch hands gone. Leaning against the kitchen counter, she asked, "So what's going on?" She saw her mother glance down the table at the marshal.

"Some poor young woman was run down in

Meadow Village last night," Dana said, getting up from the table as the timer went off on the oven. "It was a hit and run," she added, shaking her head as if in disbelief.

Mary moved out of the way as her mother grabbed a hot pad and pulled a second batch of homemade cinnamon rolls from the oven.

"You might have known her," her mother said. "She worked at that coffee shop you like."

"Lone Peak Perk?" she asked in surprise as she took a vacated seat. "I stopped by there this morning and it was closed. There was a note on the door saying there'd been a death, but I never dreamed it was anything like that. What was the woman's name?"

"Christy Shores," her father said from the head of the large kitchen table.

"Christy." She felt sick to her stomach as she called up an image of the small fair-haired young woman. Tears filled her eyes. "Oh, no. I knew her."

"Honey, are you all right?" her mother asked.

"Christy was going to move into the apartment I had available today. She'd only been working at the coffee shop for a few weeks. I can't believe she's dead. A hit and run?" she asked her father.

He nodded and glanced at his watch. "The coroner should have something more for me by now," he said, getting to his feet.

"Do you have any idea who did it?" she asked her father.

Hud shook his head. "Not yet. Unfortunately, it happened after the bars closed, and she was apparently alone walking along the side of the road dressed in all black. It's possible that the driver didn't see her."

"But whoever hit her would have known that he or she struck something," Dana said.

"Could have thought it was a deer, and that's why the person didn't stop," Hud said. "It's possible."

"And then the driver didn't stop to see what it was? Probably drunk and didn't want to deal with the marshal," Aunt Stacy mocked. "I've heard he's a real—"

"I'd watch yourself," her father said, but smiled as he took his Stetson off the hook on the wall, kissed his wife and left.

Mary took a sip of her coffee, her hands trembling as she brought the mug to her lips. It always shocked her, death and violence. She'd never understood how her father could handle his job the way he did. While there wasn't a lot of crime in the canyon, there was always something. She remembered growing up, overhearing about murders but only occasionally. Now there'd been a hit and run. Poor Christy. She'd been so excited about renting Mary's apartment, which was so close to her work. It would save her the commute from her mother's house in Bozeman, she'd said.

As the patrol SUV left, another vehicle pulled in. "Well, I wonder who that is?" she heard her mother say as she shifted in her seat to peer out the window.

Mary did the same thing, blinking in the bright morning sun at the pickup that had pulled up in front of the house almost before the dust had settled from her father leaving.

She stared as the driver's-side door opened and Chase Steele stepped out of the vehicle.

Chapter Six

"It's Chase," Mary said as if she couldn't believe it. For weeks she had dreamed of him suddenly showing up at her door. She shot a look at her mother.

"Do you need my help?" Dana asked. "If you aren't ready to talk to him, I could tell him this isn't a good time."

She shook her head and turned back to watch Chase stretch as if it had been a long drive. He looked around for a moment, his gaze softening as he took in the ranch as though, like her, he still had special memories of the place. He appeared taller, more solid, she thought as she watched him head for the front porch. Was he remembering how it was with the two of them before he left?

"I can't imagine what he's doing here," Mary said, voicing her surprise along with her worry.

Her mother gave her a pitying look. "He's here to see you."

"But why?"

"Maybe because of the letter you sent," Dana suggested.

She couldn't believe how nervous she was. This

was Chase. She'd known him since they were teens. Her heart bumped against her ribs as she heard him knock. "He could have just called."

"Maybe what he has to say needs to be said in person."

That thought scared her more than she wanted to admit. She hadn't told her mother about the call from Chase's fiancée. She'd been too embarrassed. It was enough that her aunt Stacy had told her mother about the letter she'd sent him.

"Do you want me to get that?" her mother asked when he knocked. "Or maybe you would like to answer it and let him tell you why he's here."

Another knock at the door finally made her move. Mind racing, she hurried to the door. Chase. After all this time. She had no idea what she was going to say. Worse, what *he* would say.

As she opened the door, she glanced past him to his pickup. At least he was alone. He hadn't brought the woman who'd called her, his fiancée who could by now be his wife.

"Mary."

The sound of his voice made her shift her gaze back to the handsome cowboy standing in her doorway. Her heart did a roller-coaster loop in her chest, taking all her air with it. He'd only gotten more handsome. The sleeves on the Western shirt he wore were rolled up to expose muscled tanned arms. The shirt stretched over his broad shoulders. He looked as solid as one of the large pines that stood sentinel on the mountainside overlooking the ranch.

He was staring at her as well. He seemed to catch

himself and quickly removed his Stetson and smiled. "Gosh dang, you look good."

She couldn't help but smile. He'd picked up the expression "gosh dang" from her father after Hud had caught Chase cussing a blue streak at fifteen out by their barn. The words went straight to her heart, but when she opened her mouth, she said, "What are you doing here?"

"I had to see you." He glanced past her. "I'm sorry it took me so long. My pickup broke down and... Could we talk?"

She was still standing in the doorway. She thought of her mother in the next room. "Why don't we walk down to the creek?"

"Sure," he said, and stepped back to let her lead the way.

Neither of them spoke until they reached the edge of the creek. Mary stopped in the shade of the pines. Sunlight fingered warmth through the boughs, making the rippling clear water sparkle. She breathed in the sweet familiar scents, and felt as if she needed to pinch herself. Chase.

She was struck with how different Chase looked. Stubble darkened his chiseled jawline. He was definitely taller, broader across the shoulders. There were faint lines around his blue eyes as he squinted toward the house before settling his gaze on her.

She felt heat rush to her center. The cowboy standing in front of her set off all kinds of desires with only a look. And yet after all this time, did she know this man? He'd come back. But that didn't mean that he'd come back to *her*.

"I got your letter," he said as he took off his Stetson to turn the brim nervously in his fingers.

"You didn't call or write back," she said, wondering when he was going to get to the news about the fiancée.

His gaze locked with hers. "I'm sorry but what I wanted to say, I couldn't say over the phone let alone in a letter."

Her heart pounded as she thought, *Here it comes*.

There was pain in his gaze. "I've missed you so much. I know you never understood why I had to leave. I'm not sure I understood it myself. I had to go. Just as I had to come back. I'm so sorry I hurt you." His blue-eyed gaze locked with hers. "I love you. I never stopped loving you."

She stared at him. Wasn't this exactly what she'd dreamed of him saying to her before she'd gotten the call from his fiancée? Except in the dream she would have been in his arms by now.

"What about your fiancée, Chase?"

"*Fiancée?* What would make you think—"

"She called me after I sent the letter."

He stared at her for a moment before swearing under his breath. "You talked to a woman who said she was my fiancée?"

She nodded and crossed her arms protectively across her chest, her heart pounding like a drum beneath her ribs. "Wasn't she?"

He shook his head. "Look, I was never engaged, far from it. But there was this woman." He saw her expression. "It wasn't what you think."

"I think you were involved with her."

He closed his eyes and groaned again. When he opened them, he settled those blue eyes on her. "It was one night after a party at my boss's place. It was a barbecue that I didn't even want to go to and wish I hadn't. I'd had too much to drink." He shook his head. "After that she would break into my apartment and leave me presents, go through my things, ambush me when I came home. She found your letter, but I never dreamed that she'd call you." He raked a hand through his hair and looked down. "I'm so sorry. Fiona was…delusional. She was like this with anyone who showed her any attention, but I didn't know that. I told her that night I was in love with someone else." His gaze came up to meet hers. "You. But I didn't come here to talk about her."

Fiona? Of course he had dated while he was gone. So why did hearing him say the woman's name feel as if he'd ripped out another piece of her heart? She felt sick to her stomach. "Why *did* you come here?"

"That's what I've been trying to tell you. I hated the way we left things too," Chase said. "Mary, I love you. That's why I came back. Tell me that you'll give us another chance."

"Excuse me."

They both turned to see a man silhouetted against the skyline behind them. Mary blinked as she recognized the form. "Dillon?"

Chase's gaze sharpened. "Dillon?" he asked under his breath.

"What are you doing here?" she asked, and then realized that she'd agreed to a lunch date she'd completely forgotten about because of Chase's surprising return.

"Lunch. I know I'm early, but I thought we'd go on a hike and then have lunch at one of the cafés up at the mountain resort," he said as he came partway down the slope to the creek and into the shelter of the pines. "More fun than eating at a restaurant in the village." He shrugged. "When your pickup wasn't at your office, I figured you'd be here." Dillon's gaze narrowed. "Why do I feel like I'm interrupting something?"

"Because you are," Chase said, and looked to Mary. "A friend of yours?"

"Mary and I are dating," Dillon said before she could speak. "I'm Deputy Dillon Ramsey."

"The deputy, huh," Chase said, clearly unimpressed.

Dillon seemed to grind his teeth for a moment before saying, "And you are…"

"Chase Steele, Mary's…" His gaze shifted to her.

"Chase and I grew up together here in the canyon," she said quickly as she saw the two posturing as if this might end with them exchanging blows before thrashing in the mud next to the creek as they tried to kill each other. "I didn't know Chase was… in town."

"Passing through?" Dillon asked pointedly.

Chase grinned. "Sorry, but I'm here to stay. I'm not going anywhere." He said that last part to her.

His blue eyes held hers, making her squirm for no reason she could think of, which annoyed her. It wasn't like she was caught cheating on him. Far from it since he had apparently recently dated someone named Fiona.

"If you're through here," Dillon said to her, "we should get going before it gets too hot."

"Don't let me stop you," Chase said, his penetrating gaze on her. "But we aren't finished."

"You are now," Dillon said, reaching for Mary's hand as if to pull her back up the slope away from the creek.

Chase stepped between them. "Don't go grabbing her like you're going to drag her away. If she wants to go with you, she can go under her own steam."

Dillon took a step toward Chase. "Stop," Mary cried, sure that the two were going to get physical at any moment. She looked at Chase, still shocked by his return as well as his declaration of love. "I'll talk to you later."

He smiled again then, the smile that she'd fallen in love with at a very young age. "Count on it." He stepped back and tipped his Stetson to her, then to Dillon. "I'll be around." In a few long-legged strides, he climbed the slope away from the creek.

"You coming?" Dillon asked, sounding irritated.

She sighed and started up the slope away from the creek. As they topped the hill, she saw Chase had gone to the house and was now visiting with her mother on the front porch. She could hear laughter and felt Dillon's angry reaction to Chase and her mother appearing so friendly.

He seemed to be gritting his teeth as he asked, "What's his story, anyway? He's obviously more than a friend," Dillon said as he opened the passenger-side door of his pickup and glared in Chase and Dana's direction.

"I told you, we grew up together," she said as she slid in and he slammed the door.

Dillon joined her. He seemed out of breath. For a moment he just sat there before he turned toward her. "You were lovers." It wasn't a question.

"We were high school and college sweethearts," she said.

"He's still in love with you." He was looking at Chase and her mother on the porch.

She groaned inwardly and said nothing. Of course with Chase showing up it was only a matter of time before he and Dillon crossed paths in a place as small as Big Sky. But why today of all days?

"He acts like he owns you." Dillon still hadn't reached to start the truck. Nor did he look at her. "Did he think he could come back and take up where the two of you left off?"

She'd thought the same thing, but she found herself wanting to defend Chase. "We have a history—"

He swung his head toward her, his eyes narrow and hard. "Are you getting back together?"

For a moment she was too taken aback to speak. "I didn't even know he was back in town until a few minutes ago. I was as surprised as you were, but I don't like your tone. What I decide to do is really none of your business." Out of the corner of her eye, she saw Chase hug her mother, then head for his pickup.

"Is that right?" Dillon demanded. "Good to know where I stand."

"You know, I'm no longer in the mood for a hike or lunch," she said, and reached for the door handle as Chase headed out of the ranch.

Dillon grabbed her arm, his fingers biting into her tender flesh. "He comes back and you dump me?"

"Let go of me." She said it quietly, but firmly.

He quickly released her. "Sorry. I hope I didn't— It's just that I thought you and I... And then seeing him and hearing him tell you that he was still in love with you." He shook his head, the look on his face making her weaken.

"Look, I told you. It came as a shock for me too," she said. "I don't know what I'm going to do. I'm sorry if you feel—"

"Like I was just a stand-in until your old boyfriend got back?"

"That isn't what you were."

"No?" His voice softened. "Good, because I'm not ready to turn you over to him." As he said the words, he trailed his fingers from her bare shoulder slowly down to her wrist. Her skin rippled with goose bumps and she shivered. "I still want to see that penthouse view. Can I call you later?"

She felt confused. But she knew that she wasn't in any frame of mind to make a decision about Dillon right now. She felt herself nod. "We'll talk then," she said, and climbed out of the pickup, closing the door behind her. Still rattled by everything that had happened, she stood watching him drive away, as tears burned her eyes. Chase had come back. Chase still loved her.

But there was the threatening woman who'd called

her saying she was his fiancée. Fiona. And no doubt others. And there was Dillon. Chase had no right to come back here and make any demands on her. He'd let her go for weeks without a word after he'd gotten the letter.

Chase and Dillon had immediately disliked each other, which Mary knew shouldn't have surprised her. Dillon's reaction threw her the most. Did he really have feelings for her? She felt as if it was too early. They barely knew each other. Was it just a male thing?

Still, it worried her. The two men were bound to run into each other again. Next time she might not be around to keep them from trying to kill each other.

CHASE MENTALLY KICKED HIMSELF. He should have called, should have written. But even as he thought it, he knew he'd had to do this in person. If it hadn't been for Fiona and her dirty tricks… He shook his head. He was to blame for that too and he knew it.

Well, he was here now and damned if he was going to let some deputy steal the woman he loved, had always loved.

He let out a long breath as he drove toward the ranch where he would be working until he started his carpenter job. All the way to Montana he'd been so sure that by now he'd be holding Mary in his arms.

He should have known better. He'd hurt her. Had he really thought she'd still be waiting around for him? He thought of all the things he'd planned to tell her—before that deputy had interrupted them.

Assuring himself that he'd get another chance and

soon, he smiled to himself. Mary was even more beautiful than she'd been when he left. But now there was a confidence about her. She'd come into her own. He felt a swell of pride. He'd never doubted that the woman could do anything she set her mind to.

Now all he had to do was convince her that this cowboy was worth giving a second chance.

HUD READ THROUGH the coroner's report a second time, then set it aside. Prints were still being lifted from Christy Shore's car, but the area around the battery where someone had disabled the engine had been wiped clean. Fibers had been found from what appeared to be a paper towel on the battery.

There was no doubt in his mind that Christy's death had been premeditated. Someone had tampered with her battery, needing her to walk home that night so she could be run down. Which meant that the killer must have been waiting outside the bar. Just her luck that she had stayed so late that there was no one around to give her a ride somewhere.

The killer wanted him to believe the hit and run had been an accident. He'd already heard rumors that she'd been hit by a motor home of some tourist passing through. He knew better. This was a homicide, and he'd bet his tin star that the killer was local and not just passing through.

Picking up his notebook, he shoved back his chair and stood. It was time to talk to the two men who'd fought over Christy earlier in the night. Only one name had surprised him—Grady Birch, Deputy Dillon Ramsey's friend—because the name had just come up in his cattle rustling investigation.

He decided to start with Grady, pay him a surprise visit, see how that went before he talked to the other man, Chet Jensen, the son of a neighboring rancher who'd been in trouble most of his life.

But when he reached the rented cabin outside Gallatin Gateway, Grady was nowhere around. Hud glanced in the windows but it was hard to tell if the man had skipped town or not.

MARY JOINED HER mother in a rocking chair on the front porch after Chase and Dillon had left. Dana had joked about feeling old lately, and had said maybe she was ready for a rocking chair. Mary had laughed.

But as she sat down in a chair next to her, she felt as if it was the first time she'd looked at her mother in a very long time. Dana had aged. She had wrinkles around her eyes and mouth, her hair was now more salt than pepper and there was a tiredness she'd seldom seen in her mother's bearing.

"Are you all right?" her mother asked her, stealing the exact words Mary had been about to say to her. Dana perked up a little when she smiled and reached over to take her daughter's hand.

"I saw you visiting with Chase," Mary said.

Her mother nodded. "It was good to see him. He left you his phone number." With her free hand she reached into her pocket and brought out a folded piece of notepaper and gave it to her.

She glanced at the number written on it below

Chase's name. Seeing that there was nothing else, she tucked it into her pocket. "What did he tell you?"

"We only talked about the ranch, how much the town has grown, just that sort of thing."

"He says he came back because he loves me, never stopped loving me. But I never told you this…" She hesitated. There was little she kept from her mother. "I got a call from a woman who claimed to be his fiancée. She warned me about contacting him again."

Dana's eyes widened. "This woman threatened you?"

"Chase says it was a delusional woman he made the mistake of spending one night with. Fiona." Even saying the name hurt.

"I see. Well, now you know the truth."

Did she? "I haven't forgotten why we broke up." She'd caught Chase kissing Beth Anne Jensen. He'd sworn it was the first and only time, and that he hadn't initiated it. That he'd been caught off guard. She'd known Beth Anne had had a crush on Chase for years.

But instinctively she'd also known that her parents were right. She and Chase had been too young to be as serious as they'd been, especially since they'd never dated anyone else but each other. "You try to lasso him and tie him down now, and you'll regret it," her father had said. "If this love of yours is real, he'll come back."

She'd heard her parents love story since she was a child. Her father had left and broken her mother's heart. He'd come back though and won her heart all over again. "But what if he isn't you, Dad? What if he doesn't come back?"

"Then it wasn't meant to be, sweetheart, and there is nothing you can do about that."

"Will you call him?" her mother asked now.

"I feel like I need a little space without seeing either Dillon or Chase," she said. "I still love Chase, but I'm not sure I still know him."

"It might take some time."

"I guess we'll see if he sticks around long enough to find out." She pushed to her feet. "I need to get to my office."

"I'm glad he came back," her mother said. "I always liked Chase."

Mary smiled. "Me too."

But as she drove back to her office, she knew she wouldn't be able to work, not with everything on her mind. As she pulled into her parking spot next to her building, she changed her mind and left again to drive up into the mountains. She parked at the trailhead for one of her favorite trails and got out. Maybe she'd take a walk.

Hours later, ending up high on a mountain where she could see both the Gallatin Canyon and Madison Valley on the other side, she had to smile. She was tired, sweaty and dusty, and it was the best she'd felt all day.

The hike had cleared her mind some. She turned back toward the trailhead as the sun dipped low, ignoring calls on her cell phone from both men.

DOWN THE STREET from Mary's building, Lucy studied herself in the rearview mirror of her SUV, surprised that she now actually thought of herself as Lucy. It was her new look and her ability to become someone else. It had started in junior high when she'd been asked to audition for a part in a play.

She'd only done it for extra credit since she'd been failing science. Once she'd read the part though, she'd felt herself become that character, taking on the role, complete with the accent. She'd been good, so good that she'd hardly had to try out in high school to get the leading roles.

Now as she waited, she felt antsy. Mary had come home and then left again without even getting out of her car. Lucy had been so sure that Chase would have made it to Montana by now. Waiting for him, she'd had too much time to think. What if she was wrong? What if he hadn't been hightailing it back here to his sweet little cowgirl?

What if he'd left Arizona, then changed his mind, realizing that what he had with her was more powerful than some old feelings for Mary Cardwell Savage? What if he'd gone back for her only to find out that she'd drowned and that everyone was waiting for some poor soul to find her body along the edge of the river downstream?

The thought made her heart pound. Until she remembered what she'd done to his pickup engine. Who knew where he'd broken down and how long it would take for him to get the engine fixed. If it was fixable.

No, he'd made it clear that he didn't want her. Which meant he would show up here in Big Sky. She just had to be patient and not do anything stupid.

She'd realized that she should approach this the same way she'd gone after prospective buyers in real estate. The first step was to find out what she was up against. Lucy smiled. She would get to know her enemy. She would find her weakness. She already had a plan to gain Mary's trust.

Not that she was getting overconfident. Just as important was anticipating any problems—including getting caught. With each step toward her goal, she needed to consider every contingency.

Some precautions were just common sense. She'd purchased a burner phone. She hadn't told anyone she'd known that she was alive, not even Patty. She hadn't left a paper trail. Taking all her money out of the bank before what the authorities thought was an attempted suicide had been brilliant. Just as was wearing gloves when she tampered with Christy Shores' battery.

It had been pure hell living with three older stepbrothers. But they'd taught her a lot about cars, getting even and never leaving any evidence behind. She'd used everything they'd taught her the night she burned down her stepfather's house—with her stepfather, mother and stepbrothers inside.

But sometimes she got overzealous. Maybe she'd gone too far when she'd put the bleach into Chase's engine oil. She'd considered loosening the nuts on his tires, but she hadn't wanted him to die. *Not yet.* And definitely not where she wouldn't be there.

But what if he couldn't make it to Montana now? Shouldn't he have been here by now? If he was coming. She was beginning to worry a little when she saw him. As if she'd conjured him up, he drove past where she was parked to stop in front of Mary's building. Lucy watched him park and jump out. Her heart began to pound as he strode purposely toward Mary's building to knock on the door.

Her stomach curdled as she watched him try to see into the windows before he stepped back to stare up at the top floor. "Sorry, your little cowgirl isn't home," she said under her breath. There were no lights on nor was Mary's pickup where she always parked it. But it was clear that Chase was looking for her. What would he do when he found her? Profess his undying love? As jealousy's sharp teeth took a bite out of her, she was tempted to end this now.

She'd picked up a weapon at a gun show on her way to Big Sky. All she had to do was reach under her seat, take out the loaded handgun, get out and walk over to him. He wouldn't recognize her. Not at first.

He would though when she showed him the gun she would have had hidden behind her back. "This is just a little something from Fiona." She smiled as she imagined the bullet sinking into his black heart.

But what fun would that be? Her plan was to make him suffer. The best way to do that was through his precious Mary. She'd promised herself she wouldn't deviate from the plan. No more acting on impulse. This time, she wouldn't make the same mistakes she'd made in the past.

As she watched Chase climb back into his pickup and drive away, she was trembling with anticipation at just the thought of what she had in store for the cowboy and his cowgirl.

Chapter Seven

The next morning, Mary saw that Lone Peak Perk was open again. Just the thought of one of her ultimate caramel frappaccinos made her realize it was exactly what she needed right now.

Stepping through the door, she breathed in the rich scent of coffee and felt at home. The thought made her smile. She would be in a fog all day if she didn't have her coffee and after the restless night she'd had…

As she moved to the counter, she saw that there was a new young woman working. Had they already replaced Christy? The woman's dark hair was styled in a pixie cut that seemed to accent her dark eyes. She wore a temporary name tag that had LUCY printed neatly on it.

"So what can I get you?" Lucy asked with a slight lisp and a Southern accent as she flashed Mary a wide gap-toothed smile.

"One of your ultimate caramel frappaccinos to go."

The young woman laughed. "That one's my favorite."

"I was so sorry to hear about Christy," Mary said.

"I didn't really know her." Lucy stopped what she was doing for a moment to look over her shoulder at her. "I was shocked when I realized that Christy was the one who took my application. She was nice. I couldn't believe it when I got the call. I hate that her bad luck led to my good luck. My application was on the top of the pile."

"What brought you to Big Sky?" Mary asked, seeing that she'd made the young woman uncomfortable.

"Wanderlust. I had a job waiting for me in Spokane, but I found exactly what I was looking for right here in Big Sky, Montana. Is this the most beautiful place you've ever seen?"

Mary had to smile. "I've always thought so. Where are you from? I detect an accent."

Lucy laughed. "Texas. I can't seem to overcome my roots."

"I'd keep it if I were you."

"You think?" the woman asked as she set down the go cup on the counter in front of her.

Mary nodded. "I do. I hope you enjoy it here."

"Thanks. I know I will."

CHASE WAS RELIEVED when he got the call from Mary. He'd had a lot of time to think, and he didn't want to spend any more time away from her. He'd gone over to her place last night in the hopes that they could talk. But she hadn't been home. Was she out with the deputy? The thought made him crazy.

But he had only himself to blame. He'd broken her heart when he'd left Montana. Even now though, he knew that he'd had to go. He was definitely too young for marriage back then.

But he'd grown up in the years he'd been gone. He'd learned a trade he loved. He'd seen some of the world. He wasn't the kid Mary used to hang out with. He'd known for some time what he wanted. It wasn't until he'd gotten her letter that he'd realized there was still hope. He'd been afraid that Mary had moved on a long time ago. But like him, she hadn't found anyone who tempted her into a relationship. That was until the deputy came along.

"I'm sorry about the other day, surprising you like that. You were right. I should have called."

"That's behind us," she said in a tone that let him know there was a lot more than a simple phone call to be overcome between them. He'd hurt her. Had he really thought she'd forgive him that quickly? "Just understand, I wrote that letter to tell you about the package that came for you. The rest of it was just me caught in a weak moment."

"I didn't think you had weak moments," he joked.

"Chase—"

"All I'm asking is for a chance to prove myself to you." Silence. "There's something I didn't tell you. My mother contacted me. She'd been sick off and on for years, in and out of remission. This time she was dying and wanted to see me. That's why I went to Arizona. She recently died."

"Oh, Chase, I'm so sorry. I hadn't heard."

"She asked me to bring her ashes back here. To Big Sky." He could almost hear Mary's hesitation.

"Did she…?"

"Tell me who my father was? No. I was with her the night she died. She took it to her grave."

"I'm so sorry." Mary knew how not knowing had haunted him his whole life. It was a mystery, one that had weighed him down. He wanted to know who he was, who he came from, why his mother refused to tell him. Was his father that bad? He'd known there was much more to the story, and it was a story he needed to hear.

"She did tell me one thing. She'd met the man who fathered me here in Big Sky. It's why she wanted her ashes brought back here."

"But that's all you know."

"For now. Listen—"

"I called about the package," Mary said quickly. "If your mother met your father here, well that would explain why a woman saying she was once your mother's friend left you the package. If you'd like to stop by my office to pick it up—"

"I can't come by before tomorrow. I'm working on the Jensen Ranch to earn some extra money. I had pickup trouble on the way back to town. But I was hoping we could go out—"

"I need time. Also I'm really busy."

"Is this about that deputy?" he asked, then mentally kicked himself.

"I'm not seeing Dillon right now either, not that it is any of your business. You don't get to just come back and—"

"Whoa, you're right. Sorry. I'll back off. Just know that I'm here and that I'm not going anywhere. I want you back, Mary. I've never stopped loving you and never will."

As if Mary could forget that Chase was back in town. After the phone call, she threw herself into her work, determined not to think about the handsome cowboy who'd stolen her heart years ago. Dillon kept leaving her messages. She texted him that she had a lot of work to do, and would get back to him in a day or two.

That night, she lay in bed, thinking about Chase, her heart aching. He'd hurt her, and angry, she'd broken up with him only to have him leave. She'd lost her friend and her lover. After all the years they'd spent growing up together, Mary had always thought nothing could keep them apart. She'd been wrong, and now she was terrified that she'd never really known Chase.

In the morning, she went down to work early, thankful for work to keep her mind off Chase even a little. Midmorning she looked up to see the new barista from the Lone Peak Perk standing in her doorway.

"Don't shoot me," Lucy said. "I just had a feeling you might need this." She held out the ultimate caramel frappaccino.

Mary could have hugged her. "You must be a mind reader," she said as she rose from her desk to take the container of coffee from her. "I got so busy, I actually forgot. I had no idea it was so late. I can't tell you how much I need this."

"I don't want to interrupt. I can see that you're

busy," Lucy said, taking a step toward the door. "But when I realized you hadn't been in…"

"Just a minute, let me pay you."

Lucy waved her off. "My treat. My good deed for the day." She smiled her gap-toothed smile and pushed out the door.

"Thank you so much!" Mary called after her, smiling as she watched the young woman run back across the street to the coffee shop.

Hud found Chet Jensen in the barn at his father's place just down the canyon a few miles. The tall skinny cowboy was shoveling manure from the stalls. He heard him gag, and suspected the man was hungover even before he saw his face.

"Rough night?" he asked, startling the cowboy.

Chet jumped, looking sicker from the scare. "You can't just walk up on someone like that," he snapped.

"I need to talk to you," Hud said. "About Christy Shores."

"I figured." Chet leaned his pitchfork against the side of the stall. "I could use some fresh air." With that he stumbled out of the barn and into the morning sunshine.

Hud followed him to a spot behind the ranch house where a half dozen lawn chairs sat around a firepit. Chet dropped into one of the chairs. Hud took one opposite him, and pulled out his notebook and pen.

"You heard about the fight."

He nodded. "What was that about?"

"Christy." Chet scowled across at him. "You

wouldn't be here unless you already knew that. Let's cut to the chase. I had nothing to do with her getting run over."

"Who did?"

He shrugged. "Not a clue. Beth Anne heard that a motor-home driver must have clipped her."

Hud shook his head. "I'm guessing it was someone local with a grudge. How long have you been involved with her?"

"It wasn't like that. I brought her back here a couple of times after we met a few weeks ago. I liked her."

"But?"

"But she liked Grady who was always throwing his money around, playing the big shot. I tried to warn her about him." He shook his head, then leaned over to take it in his hands.

"Are you saying you think Grady Birch might be responsible?"

"Beats me." Lifting his head, he said, "After we got thrown out of Charley's, I came home and went to bed."

"Did you see Grady leave?"

He nodded. "That doesn't mean he didn't come back."

"The same could be said about you."

Chet wagged his head. "Beth Anne was home. My sister knows I didn't leave. She was up until dawn making cookies for some special event she's throwing down at the flower shop. I couldn't have left without her seeing me."

"Christy have any enemies that you knew about?" he asked.

"I didn't think she'd been in town long enough to make enemies."

"But she'd been in town long enough to have the two of you fighting over her," he pointed out.

Chet met his gaze. "Grady and I would have been fighting over any woman we both thought the other wanted. It wasn't really even about her, you know what I mean?"

He did, he thought as he closed his notebook and got to his feet. "If you think of anyone who might have wanted her dead, call me."

Chapter Eight

Mary was just starting across the street the next morning to get her coffee when the delivery van from the local flower shop pulled up in front of her building. It had been three days since she'd seen Chase. Both men had finally gotten the message and given her space. Not that the space had helped much except that she'd gotten a lot of work done.

She groaned as she saw Beth Anne Jensen climb out of the flower shop van. "I have something for you," the buxom blonde called cheerily.

Mary couldn't remember the last time anyone had sent her flowers. Reluctantly, she went back across the street since she could already taste her ultimate caramel frappaccino. Also, the last person she wanted to see this morning was Beth Anne. The blonde had her head stuck in the back of the van as she approached.

As her former classmate came out, she shoved cellophone wrapped vase with a red rose in it at her. "I'm sure you've already heard. Chase is back."

"I know. He came by the ranch a couple of days

ago." That took some of the glee out of Beth Anne's expression.

"He's gone to work for my daddy."

Mary tried not to groan at the old news or the woman's use of "daddy" at her age. Of course, Chase had gone to work for Sherman Jensen. The Jensen Ranch was just down the road from the Cardwell spread. No wonder Chase had said he would be seeing her soon. The Jensens would be rounding up their cattle from summer range—just like everyone on Cardwell Ranch.

"Chase looks like being gone didn't hurt him none," the blonde said.

She didn't want to talk about Chase with this woman. She hadn't forgotten catching Chase and Beth Anne liplocked before he left. Mary didn't know if she was supposed to tip the owner of the flower store or not. But if it would get Beth Anne to leave… She pulled out a five and shoved it at her. "Thanks," she said, and started to turn away.

"That's not all," the blonde said as she pocketed the five and handed her a wrapped bouquet of daisies in a white vase. "Appears you've got more than one admirer." Beth Anne raised a brow.

Mary assumed that the woman knew who had sent both sets of flowers—and had probably read the notes inside the small envelopes attached to each. But then again seeing the distinct handwriting of two men on the outside of the envelopes, maybe Beth Anne was as in the dark as Mary herself. The thought improved her day.

"Have a nice day," she sang out to Beth Anne

as she headed for her office. Opening the door, she took the flowers inside, anxious to see whom they were from. She didn't want to get her hopes up. They both could be from one of the ranchers she worked for as a thank-you for the work she'd done for them.

She set down the vases on the edge of her desk and pulled out the first small envelope. Opening it, she read: "I know how you like daisies. I'm not giving up on us. Chase."

It would take more than daisies, she told herself even as her heart did a little bump against her ribs.

Shaking her head, she pulled out the other small white envelope, opened it and read: "Just wanted you to know I'm thinking of you, Dillon."

"I don't believe this," she said, and heard the front door of her building opening behind her. Spinning around, she half expected to see one or both of the men.

"Lucy," she said on a relieved breath. As touched as she was by the flowers, she wasn't up to seeing either man right now.

"Did I catch you at a bad time?" the barista asked, stopping short.

"Not at all. Your timing is perfect."

"I saw you start across the street to get your coffee and then get called back, so I thought I'd run it over to you. Your usual." She held out the cup.

"Thank you so much. I do need this, but I insist on paying you." Mary looked around for her purse. "Let me get you—"

"I put it on your account."

She stopped digging for money to look at her. "Lucy, I don't have an account."

The woman smiled that gap-toothed smile of hers that was rather infectious. "You do now. I just thought it would be easier but if I've overstepped—"

"I don't know why I hadn't thought of it, as many of these as I drink," Mary said, and raised the cup.

"I hope you don't mind. But this way, if you get too busy, just call and if we aren't busy, one of us can bring your coffee right over."

"Lucy, that's so thoughtful, but—"

"It really isn't an inconvenience. We haven't been that busy and I could use the exercise. Also it looks like you're celebrating something." She motioned to the flower delivery.

Mary laughed. "It's a long story."

"Well, I won't keep you. I better get back. It wasn't busy but it could be any minute. My shift ends soon, and I have to get back on my search for a place to live." She started to open the front door to leave.

"Lucy, wait. I have an apartment open. I haven't put up a notice that it's available. Christy was going to move in."

"The girl who died." She grimaced. "The one I replaced at Lone Peak Perk."

"Is that too weird for you?" Mary asked.

"Let me give it some thought. But could you hold on to it until later today? Thanks." And she was gone.

Mary sipped her coffee, thinking she probably shouldn't have offered the apartment without checking the young woman's references. But it was Lucy, who'd just bought her a coffee and run it across the street to her.

She turned to look at her flowers, forgetting for the moment about anything else. What was she going to do about Chase? And Dillon?

Sitting down at her desk, she picked up her phone and called her best friend, Kara, who had moved to New York after college. But they'd managed to stay in touch by phone and Facetime. It was the kind of friendship that they could go without talking for weeks and pick up right where they'd left off.

"Chase is back," she said when her friend answered.

"In Big Sky?"

"He says he loves me and that he won't give up."

Kara took a breath and let it out slowly. "How do you feel about that?"

She sighed. "I still love him, but I've been seeing someone else. A deputy here. His name is Dillon. He's really good-looking in a kind of nothing-but-trouble kind of way."

Her friend was laughing. "When it rains it pours. Seriously? You have two handsome men who are crazy about you?"

She had to laugh. "Crazy might be the perfect word. They met the other day and sparks flew. I still love Chase, but when we broke up he didn't stay and fight for me. He just left. What's to keep him from doing it again?"

"And Dillon?"

"It's too new to say. They both sent me flowers today though."

"That's a good start," Kara said with a laugh.

"Chase sent daisies because he knows I love them."

"And Dillon?"

"A rose to let me know he was thinking about me."

"Mary! Who says you have to choose between them?"

"My father doesn't like me dating either one of them."

"Which makes you want to date them even more, knowing you."

"You *do* know me," she said, and laughed again. "How are you and your adorable husband and the kids?"

"I was going to call you. I'm pregnant again!"

"Congrats," she said, and meant it. Kara was made to be a mother.

"I have morning sickness, and I'm already starting to waddle."

Mary felt a stab of envy and said as much.

"Excuse me? If anyone is envious, it's me of you. You should see me right now. Sweats and a T-shirt with a vomit stain on it—my daughter's not mine."

She laughed. "And I'll bet you look beautiful as always."

A shriek and then loud crying could be heard in the background.

"I'll let you go," Mary said. "Congrats again."

"Same to you."

She sat for a moment, idly finishing her coffee and considering her flowers before going back to work. A while later, she picked up her phone and called Chase. "Thank you for the daisies. They're beautiful. If you have some time, I thought maybe you could stop by if you're free. Like I said, I have your package here at the office. I can tell you how to find the place."

Chase chuckled. "I know how to find you. I'll be right there."

LUCY LOOKED OUT the window of the coffee shop and with a start saw Chase's truck pull up across the street. Her heart squeezed as if crushed in a large fist. Had he seen Mary before this? Had they been meeting at night on the ranch? Jealousy made her stomach roil.

Chase had been hers. At least he had until Mary wrote him that letter. She was why he'd dumped her. To come back here to his precious cowgirl. She wasn't sure at that moment whom she hated more, him or Mary, as she watched him disappear into her office.

"Excuse me?" A woman stepped in front of her, blocking her view. It was all she could do not to reach across the counter and shove her out of the way. She wanted to see what was going on across the street. "I'd like to order."

Fortunately, she got control of herself. She needed this job to get closer to Mary and pull off her plan. If she hoped to pay back Chase, she couldn't lose her cool. She plastered a smile on her face.

"I'm sorry, what can I get you?" She hadn't even realized that her Texas accent had come back until that day when she'd finally met Mary Cardwell Savage. She'd thought she'd put Texas and her childhood behind her. But apparently all of this had brought it back—along with her accent.

As she made the woman a latte, she thought about spitting in her cup, but didn't. Instead, she let herself think about the apartment in Mary's building. Of course she was going to take it. She had already gained the woman's trust. It didn't matter that Chase was over there with Mary. Soon enough she would end their little romance.

She would just have to be careful to avoid Chase. The changes in her appearance were striking, but given what they'd shared, he would know her. He would sense her beneath her disguise. He'd feel the chemistry between them. So she needed to avoid him until she was ready to make her dramatic reveal.

Smiling to herself, she considered all the ways she could make their lives miserable, before she took care of both of them. As she'd told Christy Shores, she was lucky when it came to getting what she wanted. Hadn't she gotten this job and was about to get Christy's apartment, as well?

She wanted Chase and his precious Mary to suffer. She just had to be patient.

CHASE REMOVED HIS Stetson as he stepped into Mary's office. He couldn't help but admire the building and what she'd done with it. Hardwood floors shone beneath a large warm-colored rug. The walls were recycled brick, terra-cotta in color, with paintings and photographs of the area on the walls.

"Your office is beautiful," he said. "This place suits you."

Mary smiled at the compliment, but clearly she hadn't thawed much when it came to him.

"I heard you have a couple of apartments upstairs that you rent and live on the third floor," he said. "Wise investment."

That made her chuckle. "Thank you. I'm glad you approve."

"Mary, can we please stop this?" He took a step toward her, hating this impersonal wall between them. They knew each other. Intimately. They'd once been best friends—let alone lovers.

"Thank you again for the daisies." She picked up a package from her desk and held it out to him, blocking his advance. "This is what was dropped off for you."

He chewed at the side of his cheek, his gaze on her not on the package. "Okay, if this is the way you want it. I'll wait as long as it takes." He could see that she didn't believe that. She'd lost faith in him and he couldn't blame her. For a while, he'd lost faith in himself.

"So you're working for Beth Anne's father at their ranch."

So that was it. "It's temporary. I have a job as a finish carpenter for a company that builds houses like the upscale ones here in Big Sky. It's a good job, but since it doesn't start for a week, I took what I could get in the meantime." He didn't mention that buying a new engine for his pickup had set him back some.

His gaze went to the daisies he'd had sent to her, but quickly shifted to the vase with the rose in it. "Is that from your deputy?"

MARY RAISED HER CHIN. "Don't start, Chase." She was still holding the package out to him.

He took it without even bothering to look at it. He was so close now that she could smell his masculine scent mixed with the outdoors. "I can be patient, Mary," he said, his voice low, seductive. "Remember when we couldn't keep our hands off each other?" He took another step toward her, his voice dropping even more dangerously low. "I remember the taste of you, the feel of you, the way your breath quickens when you're naked in my arms and—"

His words sent an arrow of heat to her center. "Chase—"

He closed the distance, but she didn't step back as if under the cowboy's spell. With his free hand, he ran his fingertips leisurely down her cheek to the hollow of her throat toward the V of her blouse.

She shivered and instinctively she leaned her head back, remembering his lips making that same journey. Her nipples puckered, hard and aching against her bra. "Chase—" This time, she said his name more like a plea for him not to stop.

As he pulled his hand back, he smiled. "You and I will be together again come hell or high water because that's where we belong. Tell me I'm wrong."

When she said nothing, couldn't speak, he nodded, took the package and walked out, leaving her trembling with a need for him that seemed to have grown even more potent.

Chapter Nine

Chase still hadn't paid any attention to the package Mary had given him until he tossed it on the seat of his pickup. The lightweight contents made a soft rustling sound, drawing his attention from thoughts of Mary for a moment.

As he climbed behind the wheel of his pickup, he considered what might be inside. It appeared to be an old shoebox that had been tied up with string. Both the box and the string were discolored, giving the impression of age. Why would someone leave him this? Mary had said the woman claimed to be a friend of his mother's.

His thoughts quickly returned to Mary as he drove back to the Jensen Ranch. He remembered the way she'd trembled under his touch. The chemistry was still there between them, stronger than ever. He'd wanted desperately to take her in his arms, to kiss her, to make love to her. If only she could remember how good they were together.

At the ranch, he took the shoebox inside the bunkhouse, where he was staying, tossing it on his bed. He told himself that he didn't care what was inside.

But he couldn't help being curious. He sat down on the edge of the bed and drew the box toward him. It wasn't until then that he saw the faded lettering on the top and recognized his mother's handwriting.

For Chase. Only after I'm gone.

His heart thumped hard against his ribs. This was from his mother?

He dug out his pocketknife from his jeans pocket and with trembling fingers cut the string. He hesitated, bracing himself for what he would find inside, and lifted the lid. A musty scent rose up as the papers inside rustled softly.

Chase wasn't sure what he'd expected. Old photos? Maybe his real birth certificate with his father's name on it? A letter to him telling him the things his mother couldn't or wouldn't while she was alive?

What he saw confused him. It appeared to be pages torn from a notebook. Most were yellowed and curled. His mother's handwriting was overly loopy, youthful. Nothing like her usual very small neat writing that had always been slow with painstaking precision.

He picked up one of the pages and began to read. A curse escaped his lips as he realized what he was reading. These were diary pages. His mother had left him her diary? He'd never known her to keep one.

His gaze shot to the date on the top page. It took him only a moment to do the math. This was written just weeks before he was conceived.

His pulse pounded. Finally he would know the truth about his father.

WHEN HER OFFICE door opened, Mary looked up, startled from her thoughts. Chase had left her shaken. She still wanted him desperately. But she was afraid, as much as she hated to admit it. She'd trusted her heart to Chase once. Did she dare do it again?

That's what she kept thinking even as she tried to get some work done. So when her door had opened, she was startled to realize how much time had gone by.

"Lucy." She'd forgotten all about her saying she might stop by later to discuss the apartment. Mary was glad for the distraction. "Come in."

The young woman took the chair she offered her on the other side of her desk. "Did you mean what you said earlier about renting me the apartment? It's just so convenient being right across the street, but I wanted to make sure you hadn't had second thoughts. After all, we just met."

Mary nodded since she'd *had* second thoughts. But as she looked into the young woman's eager face, she pushed them aside and reached into the drawer for the apartment key. "Why don't I show it to you." She rose from her desk. "We can either go up this way," she said, pointing to the back of her office, "or in from the outside entrance. Let's go this way." They went out of the back of her office to where a hallway wound around to the front stairs.

"The apartment is on the second floor," Mary told her as they climbed. "I live upstairs on the third floor. Some people don't want to live that close to their landlady," she said.

"I think I can handle it," Lucy said with a chuckle.

They stopped at the landing on the second floor, and Mary opened the door to the first apartment. "As you can see, it's pretty basic," she said as she pushed open the door. "Living room, kitchen, bedroom and bath." She watched Lucy take it in.

"It's perfect," the young woman said as she walked over to the window and looked out.

"There's a fire escape in the back, and a small balcony if you want to barbecue and not a bad view of Lone Peak." Mary walked to door and opened it so Lucy could see the view."

"That's perfect." She stepped past Mary out onto the small balcony to lean over the railing, before looking up. "So the fire escape goes on up to your apartment and balcony?"

"It does. I wouldn't use the fire escape except in an emergency so you will have privacy out here on your balcony."

Lucy stepped back in and closed the door. "I didn't even ask what the rent was." Mary told her. "That's really reasonable."

"I like providing housing for those working here in Big Sky. Most of the employees have to commute from the valley because there is so little affordable housing for them." She shrugged. "And it's nice to have someone else in the building at night. This area is isolated since it is mostly businesses that close by nine. The other apartment on this floor is rented to a man who travels a lot so I seldom see him."

Lucy ambled into the bedroom to pull down the Murphy bed. "This is great."

"You can use this room as an office as well as a bedroom. Since it has a closet, I call it a one bedroom."

"And it comes furnished?"

"Yes, but you can add anything you like to make it more yours."

Lucy turned to look at her. "I can really see myself living here. It's perfect. I would love it."

Mary smiled. "Then it's yours. You can move in right away if you want to."

"That's ideal because I've been staying in a motel down in the valley just hoping something opened up before I went broke."

"I'll need first and last month's rent, and a security deposit. Is that going to be a problem?"

Lucy grinned. "Fortunately, I'm not that broke yet, so no problem at all. I promise to be the perfect tenant."

Mary laughed. "I've yet to have one of those."

Back downstairs, Lucy paid in cash. Seeing her surprise, the young woman explained that she'd had the cash ready should she find a place. "They go so fast. I didn't want to miss a good opportunity. I feel as if I've hit the lottery getting first the job and now this apartment."

Mary smiled as she handed over the key. "It's nice to have you here."

"I wouldn't want to be anywhere else."

After Lucy left, Mary went back down to her office and called her mother. "I have a new tenant. It's a bit strange, but she's the barista who took Christy's place."

"That is odd. What do you know about her?"

Mary thought about it for a moment. Nothing really. "She's nice." She told her how Lucy had run across the street to bring her coffee twice when Mary had gotten busy and forgotten.

"She sounds thoughtful."

"I like her so I hope it works out." Most of her tenants had, but there was always that one who caused problems.

"Guess who sent me flowers?" she said, changing the subject and putting her new tenant out of her mind.

LUCY COULDN'T BELIEVE how easy that had been. She smiled to herself as she drove back to her motel to get her things.

Mary would be living right upstairs. It would be like taking candy from a baby. She thought of the fire escape and balconies on the two levels behind the apartment. It would be so easy to climb up to Mary's on the third floor, anytime, day or night. While there was a railing around the stairs—and the balconies—still it could be dangerous, especially if Mary had been drinking.

Her thoughts turned sour though when she recalled the two sets of flowers that had been delivered this morning. Anger set off a blaze in her chest. They had to be from Chase, right? She would have loved to have seen what he'd written on the cards. Now that she would be living in the building, maybe she would get her chance.

She still felt surprised at just how easy it had been. Then again, Mary was just too sweet for words, she thought. Also too trusting. At first, she'd just wanted to meet the woman who'd taken Chase from her. At least that's what she'd told herself. Maybe she'd planned to kill her from the very beginning. Maybe it really had been in the back of her mind from the moment she decided to go to Montana and find her—find Chase.

Her feeling had been that if she couldn't have Chase, then no one else could. She'd had dreams of killing them both. Of killing Mary and making him watch, knowing there was nothing Chase could do to save her.

But in her heart of hearts, when she was being honest with herself, she knew what she wanted was for him to fall in love with her again. Otherwise, she would have no choice. It would be his own fault. He would have to die, but only after he mourned for the loss of his precious Mary. She would kill him only after she shattered his life like he'd done hers.

Living just one floor below the woman would provide the perfect opportunity to get closer to Mary—and Chase—until she was ready to end this.

It would be dangerous. She smiled to herself.

There was nothing wrong with a little danger. Eventually she and Chase would cross paths. Lucy smiled in anticipation. She couldn't wait to see the look on his face when he realized she wasn't dead. Far from it. She'd never been more alive.

Chapter Ten

After the first sentence, Chase couldn't believe it. The pages in the shoebox were from a diary. His mother's. His fingers trembled as he picked up another page. All these years he'd wanted answers. Was he finally going to get them?

He thumbed through the random pages, looking for names. There were none. But he did find initials. He scooped up the box and pages and sat down, leaning against the headboard as he read what was written before the initials. "I woke up this morning so excited. Today was going to be wonderful. I was going to see J.M. today. He told me to meet him in our secret spot. Maybe he's changed his mind. I can only hope."

Changed his mind about what?

Chase took out another page, but it was clear from reading it that the page wasn't the next day. He began to sort them by date. Some weren't marked except by the day of the week.

But he found one that began "Christmas Day." Whoever J.M. was, his mother had been in love with the man. And since his birthday was in September—nine months from Christmas...

The entry read: "Christmas Day! I thought I wouldn't get to see him, but he surprised me with a present—a beautiful heart-shaped locket."

Chase felt his heart clench. His mother had worn such a locket. She never took it off. It was with the few things of hers that he'd kept. But he knew there was nothing but a photo of him in the locket. On the back were the words: *To my love always.*

He picked up the phone.

Mary answered on the second ring. "Chase?"

"I don't mean to bother you. But I had to tell you. It's my mother's diary."

"What's your mother's diary?"

"In the shoebox. It's pages from my mother's diary during the time that she got pregnant with me." Silence. "I really could use your help. I think the answer is somewhere in these pages but they're all mixed up. Some have dates, some don't and—"

"Bring them over. We can go through them in my apartment."

A short time later, Mary let him into the door on the side of the building, the shoebox tucked under his arm as they climbed to the third floor.

"Do you want something to drink?" she asked as he closed the door behind them.

The apartment was done in bright cheery colors that reminded him of Mary. "No, thanks." He felt nervous now that he was here.

She motioned to the dining-room table standing in a shaft of morning sun. Through the window, he could see Lone Peak. "Your apartment is wonderful," he said as he put the shoebox on the table and sat down.

"Thanks." Mary pulled out a chair opposite him. "May I?" she asked, and pulled the box toward her.

He nodded. "I looked at some of it, but truthfully, I didn't want to do this alone."

She took out the diary pages, treating them as if they were made of glass. "There had to be a reason her friend was told to give you this after she was gone." She picked up one page and read aloud, "'Friday, I saw him again at Buck's T-4. He didn't see me but I think he knew I was there. He kept looking around as if looking for me.'"

"She met him here in Big Sky!" Mary exclaimed as she flipped the page over. "'Saturday. I hate that we can't be together. He hates it too so that makes me feel a little better.'"

She looked up at Chase. "They were star-crossed lovers right here in Montana."

"Star-crossed lovers?" He scoffed. "From what I've read, it's clear that he was a married man." He raked a hand through his hair. "What if my father has been here in Big Sky all this time, and I never knew it?"

MARY COULD SEE how hard this was on him, just as she could tell that a part of him wasn't sure he wanted to know the truth. "Are you sure you want to find him?"

Chase had been fifteen when his mother had gotten sick the first time, and he'd come to the area to work on a neighboring ranch. Later, Mary's family had put him to work on their ranch, giving him a place to live while he and Mary finished school.

They'd both believed that he'd been sent to Montana because of one of Hud's law-enforcement connections. Her father had never spelled it out, but she now realized that both of her parents must have known Chase's mother back when she'd lived here. She must have been the one who'd asked them to look out for him.

Mary and Chase had been close from the very start. From as far back as she could remember, he'd been haunted by the fact that he didn't know who his father was. He'd been born in Arizona. He'd just assumed that was where his mother met his father. He hadn't known that there was much more of a Montana connection than either he or Mary had known. Until now.

"Truthfully? I'm not sure of anything." His gaze met hers. "Except how I feel about you."

"Chase—"

He waved a hand through the air. "Sorry. As for my…father… I have to know who he is and why he did what he did."

She nodded. "So we'll find him," she said, and picked up another page of the diary. "There has to be some reason he couldn't marry your mother."

He swore under his breath. "I told you. He was already married. It's the only thing that's ever made sense. It's why my mother refused to tell me who he is."

"Maybe she mentions his name on one of the

pages," Mary suggested. "If we put them in order."
She went to work, sorting through them, but quickly
realized that she never mentioned him by name, only
J.M.

She stopped sorting to look at him. "J.M.? He
shouldn't be hard to find if he still lives here." She
got up and went to a desk, returning with a laptop.
"Maybe we should read through them first though.
It doesn't look as if she wrote something every day."
She counted the diary sheets. "There are forty-two
of them with days on both sides, so eight-four days."

"About three months," Chase said. "If we knew
when the affair started…" They quickly began going
through the pages. "This might help," he said as he
held up one of the pages.

Something in his voice caught her attention more
than his words. "What is it?"

"Christmas Eve." He read what his mother had
written. "'It was so romantic. I never dreamed it could
be like this. But he reminded me that I didn't have
much to compare it with. He said it would get better.
I can't imagine.'"

Chase looked up. "I was born nine months later."

"I'm sorry," she said.

He shrugged as if it didn't matter, but it was clear
that it mattered a whole lot. "I have to know who
he is."

She heard the fury in his voice as he told her about
the heart-shaped necklace that his mother had never
taken off. "Maybe he loved her."

He scoffed at that. "If he'd loved her, he wouldn't

have abandoned her. She was alone, broke and struggling to raise his child."

"Maybe the answer is in these pages, and we just missed something," Mary said after they finished going through them.

He shook his head and scooped up the diary pages, stuffing them roughly back into the shoebox and slamming down the lid.

Mary wanted to know the whole story. She looked at the box longingly. It was clear that Chase had already made up his mind. Even after reading all the diary entries, she knew it was his mother's view of the relationship, and clearly Muriel's head had been in the stars.

"What are you going to do?" she asked, worried.

"Find him. J.M. The Big Sky area isn't that large." He stepped over to the laptop and called up local phone listings from the browser and started with the *M*s. "We can surmise from what she wrote that he's older, more experienced and married. The necklace he gave her wasn't some cheap dime-store one. He had money, probably owned a business in town."

She hesitated, worried now what he would do once he found the man in question. "I think you should let me go with you once we narrow down the list of men."

He looked at her, hope in his expression. "You would do that?"

"Of course." She picked up the phone to call her mother. Dana had known Chase's mother Muriel. That was clearly why Chase had come to live on the ranch at fifteen. "I need to know how Chase came to live with us."

She listened, and after a moment hung up and said to Chase, "Your mother worked in Meadow Village at the grocery store. She says she didn't know who Muriel was seeing, and I believe her. She would have told us if she'd known. She did say that your mother rented a place on the edge of town. So your mother could have met your father at the grocery store or on her way to work or just about anywhere around here."

Chase shook his head. "His wife probably did the grocery shopping."

"We don't know that he had a wife. We're just assuming…" But Chase wasn't listening. He was going through the phone listings.

GRADY BIRCH HAD been leaving when Hud pulled into the drive in front of the cabin. For just a moment, he thought the man might make a run for it. Grady's expression had been like a deer caught in his headlights. Hud suspected the man always looked like that when he saw the law—and for good reason.

It amused the marshal that Grady pretended nonchalance, leaning against the doorframe as if he had nothing to hide. As Hud exited his patrol SUV and moved toward the man, Grady's nerves got the better of him. His elbow slid off the doorframe, throwing the man off balance. He stumbled to catch himself, looking even more agitated.

"Marshal," he said, his voice high and strained before he cleared his throat. "What brings you out this way?"

"Why don't we step into your cabin and talk?" Hud suggested.

Grady shot a look behind him through the doorway as if he wasn't sure what evidence might be lying around in there. "I'd just as soon talk out here. Unless you have a warrant. I know my rights."

"Why would I have a warrant, Mr. Birch? I just drove out here to talk to you about Christy Shores."

Grady frowned. That hadn't been what he'd expected. The man's relief showed on his ferret-thin face. Grady's relief that this was about Christy told Hud that this had been a wasted trip. The man hadn't killed the barista. Grady was more worried about being arrested for cattle rustling.

"I just have a couple of quick questions," Hud said, hoping Grady gave him something to go on. "You dated Christy?"

"I wouldn't call it dating exactly."

"You were involved with her."

Grady shook his head. "I wouldn't say that either."

Hud sighed and shifted on his feet. "What would you say?"

"I knew who she was."

"You knew her well enough to get in a fight over her at Charley's the night she was killed."

"Let's say I had a good thing going with her, and Chet tried to horn in."

"What did Christy have to say about all this?"

Grady frowned as if he didn't understand the question. He was leaning against the doorframe again, only this time he looked a lot more comfortable.

Hud rephrased it. "What did she get out of this… relationship with you?"

"Other than the obvious?" Grady asked with a laugh. "It was a place to sleep so she didn't have to go back to her mother's in Bozeman."

"Is that where she was headed that night, to your cabin?"

Grady shook his head. "I told her it wasn't happening. I saw her making eyes at Chet. Let him put her up out at his place. I won't be used by any woman."

Hud had to bite his tongue. The way men like Grady treated women made his teeth ache. "When was the last time you saw her?"

"When Chet told her to scram and she ran into the bathroom crying."

"That was before the two of you got thrown out of the bar?" the marshal asked.

Grady nodded. "So have you found out who ran her down?"

"Not yet."

"Probably some tourist traveling through. I was in Yellowstone once, and there was this woman walking along the edge of the highway and this motor home came along. You know how those big old things have those huge side mirrors? One of them caught her in the back of the head." Grady made a disgusted sound. "Killed her deader than a doornail. Could have taken her head off if the driver had been going faster."

"Christy Shores wasn't killed by a motor home. She was murdered by someone locally."

Grady's eyes widened. "Seriously? You don't think Chet…"

"Chet has an alibi for the time of the murder. Can anyone verify that you came straight here to this cabin and didn't leave again?"

"I was alone, but I can assure you I didn't leave again."

Hud knew the value of an assurance by Grady Birch. "You wouldn't know anyone who might have wanted to harm her, do you?"

He wagged his head, still looking shocked. "Christy was all right, you know. She didn't deserve that." He sounded as if he'd just realized that if he'd brought her back to his cabin that night, she would still be alive.

DILLON WAS HEADED to Grady's when he saw the marshal's SUV coming out of the dirt road into the cabin. He waved and kept going as if headed to Bozeman, his pulse thundering in his ears. What had the marshal been doing out at the cabin? Was he investigating the cattle rustling?

He glanced in his rearview mirror. The marshal hadn't slowed or turned around as if headed back to Big Sky, and as far as Dillon could tell, Grady wasn't handcuffed in the back. He kept going until he couldn't see the patrol SUV in his rearview anymore before he pulled over, did a highway patrol turn and headed back toward the cabin.

His instincts told him not to. The marshal might circle back. Right now, he especially didn't want Hud knowing about his association with Grady Birch.

But he had to find out what was going on. If he needed to skip the state, he wanted to at least get a running start.

He drove to the cabin, parking behind it. As he did, he saw Grady peer out the window. Had he thought the marshal had reason to return? The back door flew open. Grady looked pale and shaken. Dillon swore under his breath. It must be bad. But how bad?

"What—" He didn't get to finish his question before Grady began to talk, his words tumbling over each other. He caught enough of it to realize that the marshal's visit had nothing to do with cattle. Relief washed over him.

Pushing past Grady, he went into the cabin, opened the refrigerator and took the last beer. He guzzled it like a man dying of thirst. That had been too close of a call. He'd been so sure that Hud was on to them.

"Did you hear what I said?" Grady demanded. "She was *murdered*. Marshal said so himself."

Dillon couldn't care less about some girl Grady had been hanging with, and said as much.

"You really are a coldhearted bastard," Grady snapped. "And you drank the last beer," he said as he opened the refrigerator. "How about you bring a six-pack or two out for a change? I do all the heavy lifting and you—"

"Put a sock in it or I will." He wasn't in the mood for any whining. "I have my own problems."

"The marshal sniffing around you?"

He finished the beer and tossed the can into the

corner with the others piled there. "It's the marshal's daughter. Things aren't progressing like I planned."

Grady let out a disgusting sound. "I really don't care about your love life. I've never understood why you were messing with her to start with."

"Because she could be valuable, but I don't have to explain myself to you."

His partner in crime bristled. "You know I'm getting damned tired of you talking down to me. Why don't you rustle your own cattle? I'm finished."

"Where do you think you're going?" Dillon asked, noticing a flyer on the table that he hadn't seen before. With a shock, he saw that it advertised a reward from local ranchers for any information about the recent cattle rustling.

"I'm going into Charley's to have a few, maybe pick up some money shooting pool, might even find me a woman."

"You've already jeopardized the entire operation because of the last woman you brought out here."

Grady turned to look back at him. "What are you talking about?"

"Where'd you get that notice about the reward being offered by the ranchers?"

"They're all over town."

"So you just picked up one. Did the marshal see it?"

Grady colored. "No, I wouldn't let him in. I'm not a fool."

But Dillon realized that he *was* a fool, one that he could no longer afford. "I'm just saying that maybe you should lie low."

"I was headed into town when the marshal drove up. He doesn't suspect me of anything, all right? I've got cabin fever. You stay here and see how you like it." He turned to go out the door.

Dillon picked up the hatchet from the kindling pile next to the woodstove. He took two steps and hit Grady with the blunt end. The man went down like a felled pine, his face smashing into the back porch floor. When he didn't move, Dillon set about wiping any surface he had touched on his visits. He'd always been careful, he thought as he wiped the refrigerator door and the hatchet's handle.

His gaze went to the pile of beer cans in the corner and realized that his prints were all over those cans. Finding an old burlap bag, he began to pick up the cans when he saw an old fishing pole next to the door. Smiling, he knew how he could dispose of Grady's body.

Chapter Eleven

Dillon touched Mary's cheek, making her jump. "I didn't mean to startle you. It's just that you seemed a million miles away."

Actually only five miles away, on the ranch where Chase was working.

She couldn't quit thinking about him, which is why she hadn't wanted to go out with Dillon tonight, especially after she'd told him that she needed more time.

"I guess you forgot," he'd said. "The tickets to the concert I bought after the last time we went out? You said you loved that band, and I said I should try to get us some tickets. Well I did. For tonight."

She'd recalled the conversation. It hadn't been definite, but she hadn't been up to arguing about it. Anyway, she knew that if she stayed home, all she'd do was mope around and worry about Chase.

"You've been distracted this whole night."

"Sorry," she said. "But you're right. I have a lot on my mind. Which is why I need to call it a night."

"Anything I can help you with?" he asked.

She shook her head.

"It wouldn't be some blond cowboy named Chase Steele, would it?" There was an edge to his voice. She wasn't in the mood for his jealousy.

"Chase is a friend of mine."

"Is that all?"

She turned to look at him, not liking his tone. "I can go out with anyone I want to."

"Oh, it's like that, is it?"

She reached for her door handle, but he grabbed her arm before she could get out.

"Slow down," he said. "I was just asking." He quickly let go of her. "Like you said, you can date anyone you please. But then, so can I. What if I decided to ask out that barista friend of yours?"

"Lucy?" She was surprised he even knew about her.

"Yeah, Lucy."

If he was trying to make her jealous, he was failing badly. "Be my guest," she said, and opened her door and climbed out before he could stop her again.

She heard him get out the driver's side and come after her. "Good night Dillon," she said pointedly. But he didn't take the hint.

As she pulled out her keys to open her office door, he grabbed her and shoved her back, caging her against the side of the building.

"I won't put up with you giving me the runaround."

"Let me go," she said from between gritted teeth. Her voice sounded much stronger than she felt at that moment. Her heart was beating as if she'd just run a mile. Dillon was more than wild. She could see that he could be dangerous—more dangerous than she was interested in.

CHANCE HAD BEEN parked down the street, waiting for Mary to return home. He needed to talk to her about earlier. Since getting the box his mother had left for him, he'd been so focused on finding his father that he wanted to apologize. She'd offered to help. He wanted to get it over with as soon as possible since he'd managed to narrow it down to three names.

It wasn't until he saw the pickup stop in front of her building that he realized she had been on a date with that deputy.

He growled under his breath. There was something about that guy that he didn't like. And it wasn't just that he was going out with Mary, he told himself.

Now he mentally kicked himself for sitting down the street watching her place. If she saw him, she'd think he was spying on her. He reached to key the ignition and leave when he saw the passenger door of the deputy's rig open. From where he sat, he couldn't miss the deputy grabbing Mary as she tried to get out. What the hell?

He was already opening his door and heading toward her building when he saw Dillon get out and go after her. He could tell by her body language that she wasn't happy. What had the deputy done to upset her?

Chase saw that Dillon had pinned her against the side of her building. Mary appeared to be trying to get her keys out and go inside.

"Let her go!" he yelled as he advanced on the man.

Both Mary and Dillon turned at the sound of his voice. Both looked surprised, then angry.

"This is none of your business," the two almost said in unison.

"Let go of her," he said again to the deputy.

Mary pushed free of Dillon's arms and, keys palmed, turned to face Chase as he approached. "What are you doing here?"

"I needed to talk to you, but I'm glad I was here to run interference for you. If he's giving you trouble—"

"I can handle this," she said.

Chase could see how upset she was at Dillon and now him. "Date's over. You should go," he said to the deputy.

Dillon started to come at him. Chase was ready, knowing he could take him in a fair fight. He just doubted the man had ever fought fair. Dillon threw the first punch and charged. Chase took only a glancing blow before he slugged the deputy square in the face, driving him back, but only for a moment.

The man charged again, leading with a right and then a quick left that caught Chase on the cheek. He hit Dillon hard in the stomach, doubling him over before shoving him back. The deputy sprawled on the ground, but was scrambling to his feet reaching for something in his boot when Chase heard Mary screaming for them to stop.

"Stop it!" Mary cried. "Both of you need to leave. Now."

Dillon slowly slide the knife back into its scabbard, but not before Chase had seen it. He realized how quickly the fight could have gotten ugly if Mary hadn't stopped it when she did.

The deputy got up from the ground, cussing and spitting out blood. His lip was cut and bleeding. Chase's jaw and cheek were tender. He suspected he'd have a black eye by morning.

The look Dillon gave him made it clear that this wasn't over. The next time they saw each other, if Mary wasn't around, they would settle things. At least now Chase knew what he would be facing. A man who carried a blade in his boot.

"Leave now," Mary repeated.

"We'll finish our discussion some other time," Dillon said to her pointedly, making Chase wish he knew what had been said before Mary had gotten upset and tried to go inside. Now, she said nothing as Dillon started toward his pickup.

"That man is dangerous, Mary. If he—"

She spun on him. "Are you spying on me, Chase?"

"No, I needed to talk to you. I was just waiting…" He knew he sounded lame. It had been weak to wait down the street for her.

She didn't cut him any slack. "I'm sure whatever you need to talk to me about can wait until tomorrow." She turned to open her door.

"I'm sorry," he said behind her, glad he'd been here, even though he'd made her angry. He hated to think what could have happened if he hadn't intervened.

Mary didn't answer as she went inside and closed the door.

As he walked back to his pickup, he knew he had

only himself to blame for all of this. He'd made so many mistakes, and he could add tonight's to the list.

Still, he worried. Mary thought she could handle Dillon. But the deputy didn't seem like a man who would take no for an answer.

TORN BETWEEN ANGER and fear, Mary closed and locked the door behind her with trembling fingers. What was wrong with her? Tears burned her eyes. She hadn't wanted to go out with Dillon tonight. So why had she let him persuade her into it?

And Chase. Parked down the street watching her, spying on her? She shook her head. If he thought he could come back after all this time and just walk in and start—

"Is everything okay?" asked a voice behind her, making her jump. "I didn't mean to startle you," Lucy said, coming up beside her in the hallway of her building.

Mary was actually glad to see Lucy. She'd had it with men tonight. She wiped her eyes, angry at herself on so many levels, but especially for shedding more tears over Chase. Her life had felt empty without him, before Dillon, but now she missed that simple world.

Even as she told herself that, she knew she was lying. Chase was back. She loved him. She wanted him. So why did she keep pushing him away?

"What was that about?" Lucy asked, wide-eyed as they both watched the two men leave, Dillon in a hail of gravel as he spun out, and Chase limping a little as he headed for his truck.

"Nothing," she said, and took a deep breath before letting it out. She was glad to have Lucy in the building tonight.

Lucy laughed. "*Nothing?* They were fighting over you. Two men were just fighting over you." She was looking at her with awe.

Mary had to smile. "It had more to do with male ego than me, trust me." She thought about saying something to Lucy about Dillon's warning to Mary that he'd ask her out, but realized it was probably a hollow threat. Anyway, she was betting that Lucy could take care of herself.

LUCY TRIED TO keep the glee out of her voice. She'd witnessed the whole thing. Poor Chase. What struck her as ironic was that she'd had nothing to do with any of it. This was all Mary's own doing.

"Would you like to come up to my apartment for a drink? Sometimes I've found talking also helps." She shrugged.

Mary hesitated only a moment before she gave Lucy an embarrassed smile. "Do you have beer?"

Lucy laughed. "Beer, vodka, ice cream. I'm prepared for every heartbreak."

They climbed the stairs, Lucy opened the door and they entered her apartment. "I haven't done much with the space," Lucy said as she retrieved two beers from the refrigerator and handed one to Mary. "But I'm excited to pick up a few things to make it more mine. It really doesn't need anything. You've done such a good job of appointing it."

"Thank you," Mary said, taking the chair in the

living room. "I'm just glad you're enjoying staying here. I'm happy to have you." Mary took a sip of her beer, looking a little uneasy now that she was here.

Lucy curled her legs under her on the couch, getting comfortable, and broke the ice, first talking about decorating and finally getting to the good part. "I had to laugh earlier. I once had two men fight over me. It was in high school at a dance. At the time I'd been mortified with embarrassment." She chuckled. "But my friends all thought it was cool."

"That was high school. It's different at this age," Mary said, and took another drink of her beer.

Lucy cocked her head at her as she licked beer foam from her lips and got up to get them another. "But I'm betting there was one of those men who you wanted to win the fight for you."

Mary looked surprised, then embarrassed.

"I wager it wasn't the deputy."

"You're right," her landlady admitted as she took the second beer. "Chase was my first love since the age of fifteen when he came to Montana to work on the ranch. We became best friends before…" Mary mugged a face. "Before we fell in love."

"So what happened to your happy ending?" Lucy asked as she took her beer back to the couch. She leaned toward Mary expectantly.

"I caught him kissing another woman. He swore the woman kissed him, but I guess I realized then that maybe what my parents had been saying was true. We were too young to be that in love. Only twenty-four. I let Chase go. He left Montana to…find himself," Mary said, and took another sip.

"*Find himself?* I'm guessing you didn't know he was lost."

Mary shook her head with a laugh. "We *were* too young to make any big decisions until we'd lived more. My father said that I had to let Chase sow some wild oats. But I didn't want him to leave."

Lucy groaned. "If he wanted to date other women, you didn't really want him to do it here, did you?"

"I wanted him to tell me that he didn't need to go see what else was out there. That all he wanted was me. But he didn't."

"And now it's too late?"

Mary shook her head. "I still love him."

Lucy traced her fingers around the top of her beer can for a moment. "Why do you think he came back now?"

Mary shook her head. "It's my fault." She sighed. "Have you ever had a weak moment when you did something stupid?"

She laughed. "Are you kidding? Especially when it comes to men."

"I found his address online since I didn't have his cell phone number or email, and he wasn't anywhere on social media. I wrote him a letter, late at night in a nostalgic mood." Mary shook her head. "Even as I wrote it, I knew I'd never mail it."

This was news. "You didn't mail it?"

"I did put it in an envelope with his address on it. I was staying out at the ranch because my horse was due to have her colt that night. I forgot about the letter—until I realized it was gone. My aunt Stacy saw it and thought I meant to mail it, so she did it for me."

Lucy leaned back, almost too surprised to speak. "So if your aunt hadn't done that…"

Mary nodded. "None of this would have probably happened, although Chase says he was planning to come back anyway. But who knows?"

The woman had no idea, Lucy thought. "So, he's back and he's ready to settle down finally?"

"I guess."

She sipped her beer for a moment. "Is that what you want?"

"Yes, I still love him. But…"

"But there is that adorable deputy," Lucy said with a laugh. "Sounds like a problem we should all have. And it's driving Chase crazy with jealousy."

"You're right about that. He can hardly be civil to Dillon when they cross paths. He says there's something about the guy that he doesn't trust."

"Obviously, he doesn't want you dating the guy."

"I'm not going out with Dillon again, and it has nothing to do with what Chase wants. I didn't date for a long time after Chase left. I was too heartbroken. I finally felt ready to move on, and I wrote that stupid letter." She drained her beer, and Lucy got up to get her another.

"What about you?" Mary asked, seeming more comfortable now that she'd gotten that off her chest and consumed two beers.

"Me?" Lucy curled up on the couch again. "There

was someone. I thought we were perfect for each other. But in the end, I was more serious than he was." She shook her head. "You know what I think is wrong with men? They don't know what they want. They want you one day, especially if there is another guy in the picture, but ultimately how can you trust them when the next minute they're waffling again? Aren't you afraid that could happen if Dillon is out of the picture?"

Mary shook her head. "I'd rather find out now than later. Trust. That is what it comes down to. Chase broke my trust when he left, when he didn't answer my letter right away or even bother to call." She seemed to hesitate. "There was this woman he was seeing."

Her ears perked up. "He told you about her?"

"He had to after I told him that she'd called me. Apparently, she'd read my letter to him. She called to tell me to leave him alone because they were engaged."

"Were they?"

"No, he says that she's delusional."

"Wow, it does sound like she was emotionally involved in a big way. He must have cared about her a little for her to react that way."

Mary shrugged. "I know he feels guilty. He certainly didn't want her to die. He admitted that he slept with her one night. But that now just the sound of her name is like fingernails on a blackboard for me. *Fiona*." She dragged out the pronunciation of the name.

Lucy laughed. "*He even told you her name?* Men. Sometimes they aren't very smart. Now you'll always wonder about her and if there is more to the story."

Chapter Twelve

Mary couldn't remember the last time she'd drunk three beers. But as she'd taken the stairs to her third-floor apartment, she'd been smiling. She'd enjoyed the girl-time with Lucy. It made her realize how cut off she'd been from her friends.

A lot of them had moved away after college, and not come back except for a week at Christmas or in the summer. They'd married, had children or careers that they had to get back to. Even though they often promised to stay in touch, they hadn't. Life went on. People changed.

Mary also knew that some of them thought staying in a place where they'd grown up had a stigma attached to it as if, like Chase, they thought the grass was greener away from Big Sky, away from Montana. They went to cities where there were more opportunities. They had wanted more. Just like Chase.

They had wanted something Mary had never yearned for. Everything she needed was right here, she told herself as she drove out to the ranch. She'd wandered past the state line enough during her college days that she knew there was nothing better out there than what she had right here.

So why hadn't she been able to understand Chase's need to leave? Why had she taken it so personally? He'd wanted her to go with him, she reminded herself. But she'd had no need to search for more, not realizing that losing Chase would make her question everything she held dear.

Mary found her mother in the kitchen alone. The moment Dana saw her she said, "What's wrong?"

She and her mother had always been close. While her male siblings had left Montana, she'd been the one to stay. Probably since she'd been the one most like her mother and grandmother.

"Nothing really," she said as she poured herself a cup of coffee and dropped into a chair at the large kitchen table. Sunshine streamed in the open window along with the scent of pine and the river. "Can't I just come by to see my mother?"

Dana cocked an eyebrow at her.

She sighed and said, "It's *everything*. Chase's mother left him this shoebox with diary pages from what appears to be the time she became pregnant with him."

"About his father? That's why you called me and asked me if I knew. Isn't his name in the diary pages?"

She shook her head. "Muriel didn't mention his name, just his initials, J.M. Does that ring any bells?"

"No, I'm sorry. I didn't know Muriel well. I'd see her at the grocery store. She came out to the ranch a couple of times. We went horseback riding. Then I heard that she'd left town. Fifteen years later, she contacted me, thanked me for my kindness back when she lived in Big Sky and asked for our help with Chase."

Mary nodded. "Well, we know why she left. It appears her lover might have been married or otherwise unavailable."

"That would explain a lot," Dana said. "How is Chase taking all of this?"

Mary shook her head. "Not well. He's determined to find him. But with only the man's initials…"

"That's not much help I wouldn't think."

"I'm afraid what he'll do when he finds him," Mary said. "He has such animosity toward him."

"It's understandable. If the man knew Muriel was pregnant and didn't step up, I can see how that has hurt Chase. But is that what happened?"

"That's just it. We don't know. Either she didn't include the diary pages at the end or she never wrote down what happened. The last page we found she was going to meet him at their special place and was very nervous about telling him the news. But that she believed their love could conquer anything."

Dana shook her head. "So Chase is assuming she told him and he turned her away."

Mary nodded. "It's the obvious assumption given that his mother refused to tell him anything about his father."

Dana got up to refill her cup. When she returned

to the table, she asked, "How was your date with Dillon last night?"

Mary looked away. "I'm not going out with him again."

"Did something happen?" Dana sounded alarmed, and Mary knew if she didn't downplay it, her mother would tell her father, and who knew what he would do. He already didn't like Dillon.

"It was fine, but that's the problem. He's not Chase." Her mother was giving her the side-eye, clearly not believing any of it.

She realized that she had to give her more or her mother would worry. "Dillon doesn't like me seeing Chase."

"I see." She probably did. "So that's it?"

She nodded. "Chase isn't wild about me seeing Dillon, but he's smart enough not to try to stop me." Mary tried to laugh it all off as she got up to take her cup to the sink. "Kara says it's a terrible problem to have, two men who both want me."

"Yes," her mother said. "If Dillon gives you a hard time—"

"Do not say a word to Dad about this. You know how he is. I just don't want to go out with Dillon again. That should make Dad happy."

"Only if it is your choice."

"It is. I need to get to work."

Dana got up to hug her daughter before she left. "We just want you to be happy. Right now it doesn't sound like either man is making you so."

"His mother's diary has blindsided Chase, but it would anyone. This whole mystery about who his father is…" She glanced at the clock. "I have to get going. Remember, nothing about this to Dad."

Her mother nodded even though Mary knew there were few secrets between them.

LUCY COULDN'T HAVE been more pleased with the way things had gone last night. Mary had been furious with Chase. The cowboy had done it to himself. *Fiona* hadn't even had a hand in it.

She was still chuckling about it this morning when the bell over the coffee shop door jangled and she turned to see the deputy come in.

Dillon Ramsey. She immediately picked up a vibe from him that made her feel a kinship. They might have more in common than Mary.

"Good morning," she said, wondering what kind of night he'd had after everything that had happened. How serious was he about Mary? Not that much, she thought as he gave her the eye. He had a cut lip and bruise on his jaw, but he didn't seem any the worse for wear.

"What can I get you?" she asked, and he turned on a grin that told her he'd come in for more than coffee. What was this about?

"I'd take a coffee, your choice, surprise me."

Oh, she could surprise him in ways he never dreamed of. But she'd play along. "You got it," she said, and went to work on his coffee while he ambled over to the window to stare across the street at Mary's building.

She made him something strong enough to take

paint off the walls, added a little sweetness and said, "I think I have just what you need this morning."

He chuckled as he turned back to her. "I think you're right about that." He blatantly looked her up and down. "Go out with me."

Okay, she hadn't been expecting that. But all things considered, the idea intrigued her. "I'm sorry, but aren't you dating my landlady?"

"Who says I can't date you too?"

She raised an eyebrow. Clearly, he wanted to use her to make Mary jealous. He could mess up her plans. She couldn't let him do that. Realizing he could be a problem, she recalled that Mary had plans tonight so she wouldn't be around.

"I'll tell you what. I'm working the late shift tonight. I wouldn't be free until midnight." She wrote down the number of her burner phone and handed him the slip of paper. "Why don't you give me a call sometime."

He grinned as he paid for his coffee. "I'll do that."

Lucy grinned back. "I'm looking forward to it," she said, meaning it. Dillon thought he could use her. The thought made her laugh. He seriously had no idea who he was dealing with.

MARY LOOKED UP as Chase came in the front door of her building.

He held up his hands in surrender. "I don't want to keep you from your work, but I thought maybe we could have lunch together if you don't have other plans. I really need to talk to you. Not about us. You asked for space, and I'm giving it to you. But I do need your help."

She glanced at her watch, surprised to see that it was almost noon. Which meant that all the restaurants would be packed. She said as much to him.

He grinned, which was always her undoing with him. "I packed us a picnic lunch. I know you're busy, so I thought we would just go down by the river. I'll have you back within the hour. If it won't work out, no sweat. I'll leave."

She hadn't been on a picnic in years. But more important, Chase wasn't pressuring her. There was a spot on the river on the ranch that used to be one of their favorite places. The memory of the two of them down by the river blew in like a warm summer breeze, a caress filled with an aching need.

"It's a beautiful day out. I thought you could use a little sunshine and fresh air," he said.

She glanced at the work on her desk. "It is tempting." *He* was tempting.

"I didn't just come here about lunch," he said as if confessing. "I've narrowed down the search for my father to three names." That caught her attention. "I was hoping—"

"Just give me a minute to change."

They drove the short distance to the Gallatin River and walked down to a spot with a sandy shore. A breeze whispered in the pines and off the water to keep the summer day cool.

Chase carried a picnic basket that Mary knew he'd gotten from her mother. "Was this my mother's idea?"

He laughed. "I do have a few ideas of my own." His blue gaze locked with hers, sending a delicious shiver through her. She remembered some of his ideas.

She sighed and took a step away from him. Being so close to Chase with him looking at her like that, she couldn't think straight. "It makes me nervous, the two of you with your heads together." When he said nothing, she'd looked over at him.

He grinned. She did love that grin. "Your mom and I have always gotten along great. I like her."

She eyed him for a moment and let it go. Did he think that getting closer to her mother was going to make her trust him again? "How is work going on the Jensen Ranch?"

"I've been helping with fencing so if you're asking about Beth Anne? I haven't even seen her." He shook his head. "Like I told you, it's temporary. I start as finish carpenter with Reclaimed Timber Construction next week. I'll also be moving into my own place in a few days. I was just helping out at the Jensens' ranch. Since I left, I've saved my money. I'm planning to build my own home here in the canyon." He shrugged and then must have seen her surprised expression. "Mary, I told you, I'm not leaving. I love you. I'm going to fight like hell to get you back. Whatever it takes. Even if I have to run off that deputy of yours."

"Don't talk crazy." She noticed the bruise on his cheek from last night reminding her of their fight.

"Seriously, there is something about him I don't like."

"That was obvious, but I don't want to talk about him. Especially with you."

"Not a problem," he said as he spread out a blanket in the sand and opened the picnic basket "Fresh lemonade. I made it myself."

"With my mother's help," she said as he held up the jug. She could hear the ice cubes rattling.

"I know it's your favorite," he said as he produced a plastic glass and poured her some. As he handed it to her, he smiled. "You look beautiful today, by the way."

She took the glass, her fingers brushing against his. A tingle rushed through her arm to her center in a heartbeat. She took a sip of the lemonade. "It's wonderful. Thank you."

"That's not all." He brought out fried chicken, potato salad and deviled eggs.

"If I eat all this, I won't get any work done this afternoon," she said, laughing.

"Would that be so terrible?"

She smiled at him as she leaned back on the blanket. The tops of the dark pines swayed in the clear blue overhead. The sound of the flowing clear water of the Gallatin River next to them was like a lullaby. It really was an amazing day, and it had been so long since she'd been here with Chase.

"I haven't done this since…"

"I left. I'm sorry."

"Not sorry you left," she said, hating that she'd brought it up.

"Just sorry it wasn't with you."

She nodded and sat up as he handed her a plate. "I guess we'll never agree on that."

"Maybe not. But we agree on most everything else," he said. "We want the same things."

"Do we?" she asked, meeting his gaze. Those old feelings rushed at her, making her melt inside. She loved this cowboy.

"We do. Try the chicken. I fried it myself."

She took a bite and felt her eyes widen. "It's delicious." It wasn't her mother's. "There's a spice on it I'm having trouble placing."

"It's my own recipe."

"It really is good."

"I wish you didn't sound so surprised." But he grinned as he said, "Now the potato salad."

"Equally delicious. So you cook?"

His face broke in a wide smile. "You really underestimate me. Cooking isn't that tough."

They ate to the sound of the river, the occasional birdsong and the chatter of a distant squirrel. It was so enjoyable that she hated to bring up a subject that she knew concerned him. But he'd said he needed to talk to her about the names of men he thought might be his father.

"You said you've narrowed your search to three names?" she asked.

He nodded. "J.M. I've searched phone listings.

Since it was someone in the Big Sky area that helps narrow the scope."

Unless the man had just been passing through. Or if he'd left. But she didn't voice her doubts. "What is your plan? Are you going to knock on the door of the men with the initials J.M.?"

He laughed. "You have a better suggestion?"

She studied him. "You're sure you want to do this?"

Chase looked away for a moment. "I wish I could let it go. But I have to know."

"What will you do when you find him?"

He chuckled. "I have no idea."

"I don't believe that."

Chase met her gaze. "This man used my mother and when she got pregnant, he dumped her."

"That isn't what she said in her diary."

"No, she didn't spell it out, if that's what you mean. But I know how it ended. With her being penniless trying to raise me on her own. It's what killed her, working like a dog all those years. I want to look him in the face and—" His voice broke.

She moved to him. As he drew her into his arms, she rested her head against the solid rock wall of his chest. She listened to the steady beat of his heart as tears burned her eyes. She knew how important family was. She'd always known hers. She could feel the hole in his heart, and wanted more than anything to fill it. "Then let's find him."

As they started to pack up the picnic supplies, Chase took her in his arms again. "You know I've never been that good with words."

"Oh, I think you're just fine with words," she said, and laughed.

"I love you," he said simply.

She met his gaze. Those blue eyes said so much that he didn't need words to convince her of that. "I love you."

"That's enough. For now," he said, and released her. The promise in his words sent a shiver of desire racing through her. Her skin tingled from his touch as well as his words. She'd wanted this cowboy more than she wanted her next breath.

Still, she let him finish picking up the picnic supplies. He smiled at her. "Ready?"

Just about, she thought.

LUCY HAD BEEN shocked when Chase had stopped by Mary's and the two had left together. She'd thought Mary was angry with him. Clearly, not enough.

Where had they been? Not far away because he'd brought her back so soon. But something was different. She could sense it, see it in the way they were with each other as he walked her to her door. They seemed closer. She tried to breathe. Her hands ached from being balled up into fists.

Watching from the window of the coffee shop, she saw Mary touch his hand. Chase immediately took hers in his large, sun-browned one. The two looked at each other as if... As if they shared a secret. Surely they weren't lovers again already. Then Chase kissed her.

Lucy brought her fist down on the counter. Cups rattled and Amy, who'd been cashing out for the day, looked over at her. "Sorry. I was trying to kill a pesky fly."

Amy didn't look convinced, but she did go back to what she was doing, leaving Lucy alone to stare out the window at the couple across the street. Chase had stepped closer. His hands were now on her shoulders. Lucy remembered his scent, his touch. He was hers. Not Mary's.

Chase leaned in and kissed her again before turning back to his pickup. It wasn't a lover's kiss. It was too quick for that. But there was no doubt that Mary was no longer angry with him. Something had changed.

She watched him drive away, telling herself to bide her time. She couldn't go off half-cocked like she had that night at the river. Timing was everything.

A customer came in. She unfisted her hands as she began to make the woman's coffee order and breathe. But she kept seeing the way Chase had kissed his cowgirl and how Mary had responded. It ate at her heart like acid, and she thought she might retch.

But she held it together as the coffee shop filled with a busload of tourists. Soon Mary would come over for her afternoon caffeine fix. Lucy touched the small white package of powder in her apron pocket. She was ready for her.

MARY TRIED TO concentrate on her work. She had to get this report done. But her mind kept going back to Chase and the picnic and the kisses.

She touched the tip of her tongue to her lower

lip and couldn't help but smile. Some things didn't change. Being in Chase's arms again, feeling his lips on hers. The short kiss was a prelude to what could come.

"Don't get ahead of yourself," she said out loud. "You're only helping him look for his father." But even as she said it, she knew today they'd crossed one of the barriers she'd erected between them.

She shook her head and went back to work, losing herself in the report until she heard her front door open. Looking up, she saw Lucy holding a cup of coffee from Lone Peak Perk.

"I hope I'm not disturbing you," she said. "When it got late, I realized you might need this." She held out the cup.

"What time is it?"

"Five thirty. I'm sorry. You probably don't want it today." She started to back out.

"No, it's just what I need if I hope to get this finished today," Mary said, rising from her desk. "I lost track of time and I had a big lunch. It's a wonder I haven't already dozed off."

Lucy smiled as she handed her the coffee. "I saw your cowboy come by and pick you up. Fun lunch?"

Mary nodded, grinning in spite of herself. "Very fun." She reached for her purse.

"I put it on your account."

She smiled. "Thank you." She took a sip. "I probably won't be able to sleep tonight from all this sugar and caffeine this late in the day, but at least I should be able to get this report done now. Thank you again. What would I do without you?"

Chapter Thirteen

Mary thought she was going to die. She'd retched until there was nothing more inside her, and yet her stomach continued to roil.

When it had first hit, she'd rushed to the restroom at the back of her office. She'd thought it might have been the potato salad, but Chased had ice packs around everything in the basket.

Still, she couldn't imagine what else it could have been. Flu? It seemed early in the season, but it was possible.

After retching a few times, she thought it had passed. The report was almost finished. She wasn't feeling great. Maybe she should go upstairs to her apartment and lie down for a while.

But it had hit again and again. Now she sat on the cool floor of the office bathroom, wet paper towels held to her forehead, as she waited for another stomach spasm. She couldn't remember ever feeling this sick, and it scared her. She felt so weak that she didn't have the strength to get up off this floor, let alone make it up to her third-floor apartment.

She closed her eyes, debating if she could reach

her ~~desk~~ where she'd left her cell phone. If she could call her mother…

"Mary? Mary, are you here?"

Relieved and afraid Lucy would leave before she could call her, Mary crawled over to the door to the hallway and, reaching up, her arm trembling, opened it. "Lucy." Her throat hurt. When her voice came out, the words were barely audible. "Lucy!" she called again, straining to be heard since she knew she couldn't get to her feet as weak as she was.

For a moment it seemed that Lucy hadn't heard her. Tears burned her eyes, and she had to fight breaking down and sobbing.

"Mary?"

She heard footfalls and a moment later Lucy was standing over her, looking down at her with an expression of shock.

"I'm sick."

"I can see that." Lucy leaned down. "Do you want me to call you an ambulance?"

"No, if you could just help me up to my apartment. I think it must be food poisoning."

"Oh no. What did you have for lunch?" Lucy asked as she reached down to lift her into a standing position. "You're as weak as a kitten."

Mary leaned against the wall for a moment, feeling as if she needed to catch her breath. "Chase made us a picnic lunch. It must have been the chicken or the potato salad."

"That's awful. Here, put your arm around me. Do you think you can walk?"

They went out the back of the office and down the hallway to the stairs.

"Let me know if you need to rest," Lucy said as they started up the steps.

Her stomach empty, the spasms seemed to have stopped—at least for the moment. Having Lucy here made her feel less scared. She was sure that she'd be fine if she could just get to her apartment and lie down.

"I'm all right." But she was sweating profusely by the time they'd reached her door.

"I didn't think to ask," Lucy said. "Are your keys downstairs?"

Mary let out a groan of frustration. "On my desk."

"If you think you can stand while I run back down—"

"No, there's a spare key under the carpet on the last stair at the top," she said. "I sometimes forget when I just run up from the office for lunch."

"Smart."

She watched Lucy retrieve the key. "I can't tell you how glad I was to see you."

"I saw that your lights were still on in your office, but there was no sign of you. I thought I'd better check to make sure everything was all right. When I found your office door open and you weren't there…" She opened the door and helped her inside.

"I think I want to go straight to my bedroom. I need to lie down."

"Let me help you." Lucy got her to the bed. "Can you undress on your own?"

"If you would just help me with my boots, I think I can manage everything else."

Lucy knelt down and pulled off her Western boots. "Here, unbutton your jeans and let me pull them off. You'll be more comfortable without them."

Mary fumbled with the buttons, realizing the woman was right. She felt so helpless, and was grateful when Lucy pulled off her jeans and helped tuck her into bed. "Thank you so much."

"I'm just glad I could help. Would you like some ginger ale? My mother always gave me that when I had a stomachache."

Mary shook her head. "I think I just need to rest."

"Okay, I'll leave you to it. I don't see your phone."

"It's downstairs on my desk too."

"I'll get it so you can call if you need anything, and I mean anything, you call me, all right? I'll be just downstairs."

Mary nodded. Suddenly she felt exhausted and just wanted to close her eyes.

"Don't worry. I'll lock your apartment door, put the key back, lock up downstairs—after I get your phone. You just rest. You look like something the cat dragged in."

Even as sick as she was, Mary had to smile because she figured that was exactly what she looked like given the way she felt.

Lucy started to step away from the bed, when Mary grabbed her hand. "Thank you again. You're a lifesaver."

"Yep, that's me."

Unable to fight it any longer, Mary closed her eyes, dropping into oblivion.

LUCY HAD TAKEN her time earlier when she'd finished work. She'd casually crossed the street, whistling a tune to herself. There'd been no reason to hurry. She'd known exactly what she was going to find when she got to Mary's office.

Now as Mary closed her eyes, she stood over the woman, simply looking down into her angelic face. She didn't have to wonder what Chase saw in Mary. She was everything Lucy was not.

That was enough to make her want to take one of the pillows, force it down on Mary's face and hold it there until the life ebbed out of her.

She listened to Mary's soft breaths thinking how Mary had it all. A business, a building in a town where she was liked and respected, not to mention rentals and Chase. Lucy reminded herself that she used to have a great profession, where she was respected, where she had friends. What was missing was a man in her life. Then along came Chase.

With a curse, she shook her head and looked around the room as she fought back tears. The bedroom was done in pastel colors and small floral prints, so like Mary. She wondered what Chase thought of this room—or if he'd seen it yet. Not very manly. Nor was it her style, she thought as she left, closing the bedroom door softly behind her, and checked out the rest of the place.

She'd been sincere about Mary's decorating abilities. The woman had talent when it came to design and colors. It made her jealous as she took in the living room with its overstuffed furniture in bright cheery colors. Like the bedroom, there was a soft comfort about the room that made her want to curl up in the chair by the window and put her feet up.

But with a silent curse, she realized that what she really wanted was to be Mary Savage for a little while. To try out her life. To have it all, including Chase.

Shaking herself out of such ridiculous thinking, she left the apartment, leaving the door unlocked. As she put the spare key back, she told herself that it would come in handy in the future.

Smiling at the thought, she headed downstairs to Mary's office. It looked like any other office except for the large oak desk. The brick walls had been exposed to give the place a rustic look. The floor was bamboo, a rich color that went perfectly with the brick and the simple but obviously expensive furnishings.

She would have liked an office like this, she thought as she found Mary's cell phone on her desk and quickly pocketed it before picking up the woman's purse. It felt heavy. She heard the jingle of keys inside. Slipping the strap over her shoulder, she went to the front door and locked it.

Across the street she saw that the coffee shop was still busy and the other baristas were clearly slammed with orders. She wondered if anyone had seen her and quickly left by the back way again, turning out the lights behind her after locking the door. That's when she realized that she couldn't kill Mary here. She would be the first suspect.

Once on the stairs, out of view of anyone outside or across the street, she sat down on a step and went through Mary's purse. She found a wallet with photos of people she assumed must be relatives. Brothers and sisters? Cousins? Her parents?

Friends? She realized how little she knew about the woman.

There was eighty-two dollars in cash in the wallet, a few credit cards, some coupons… Seriously? The woman clipped coupons? Other than mints, a small hairbrush, a paperback and miscellaneous cosmetics there was nothing of interest.

She turned to Mary's cell phone.

Password protected. Swearing softly, she tried various combinations of words, letters, numbers. Nothing worked.

A thought struck her like a brick. She tried Chase. When that didn't work, she tried Chase Steele. Nope.

She had another thought, and taking the keys to the office, she went back inside. Turning on a small lamp on the desk, she quickly began a search. She found the list of passwords on a pull-out tray over the right-hand top drawer. The passwords were on an index card and taped down. Some had been scratched out and replaced.

Lucy ran her finger down until she found the word cell. Next to it was written Homeranch#1. She tried the password and the phone unlocked.

Quickly she scanned through contacts, emails and finally messages. She found a cell phone number for Chase and on impulse tried it, just needing to hear his voice.

It was no longer in service.

Surely he had a cell phone, not that she'd ever had his number. Wouldn't he have given it to Mary though?

She went through recent phone calls, and there it was. She touched the screen as she memorized the number. It began to ring. She held her breath. He would think it was Mary calling. He would call back.

Lucy quickly hit the hang-up button but not quick enough. "Hello, Mary, I was just thinking of you." She disconnected, wishing she hadn't done that. He'd sounded so happy that Mary was calling him that she felt sick to her stomach.

Just as she'd feared, he called right back. She blocked his call. He tried again. What if he decided to come check on Mary? This was the kind of mistake she couldn't make.

She answered the phone, swallowed and did her best imitation of Mary's voice, going with tired and busy. "Working. Didn't mean to call."

"Well, I'm glad you did. Don't work too late."

"Right. Talk tomorrow." She disconnected, pretty sure she'd pulled it off. He wouldn't question the difference in their voices since he'd called Mary's phone. At least she hoped she'd sounded enough like the woman. Sweet, quiet, tired, busy. When the phone didn't ring again, she told herself that she'd done it.

Hurrying back upstairs, she picked up Mary's

purse from where she'd left it on the step on her way. Outside the third-floor apartment, she stopped to catch her breath. Putting Mary's cell on mute, she carefully opened the door, even though she didn't think Mary would be mobile for hours.

An eerie quiet hung in the air. She stepped in and headed for the bedroom. The door was still closed. She eased it open. The room had darkened to a shadowy black with the drapes closed. Mary lay exactly where she'd left her, breathing rhythmically.

Taking the cell phone, she stepped in just far enough to place the now turned off phone next to her bed. Then she left, easing the bedroom door closed behind her. The apartment was deathly quiet and growing darker. It no longer felt cozy and she no longer wanted to stay. Leaving Mary's purse on the table by the door, she left, locking it behind her.

It had been an emotional day, Lucy thought. She took the stairs down to her apartment, unlocked her door and, turning on a light, stepped in. The apartment was in stark contrast to Mary's. While everything was nice, it was stark. Cold.

"That's because you're cold," she whispered as she locked the door behind her. "Anyway, it's temporary." But even as she said it, she was thinking that she should at least buy a plant.

The apartment had come furnished right down to two sets of sheets and two throw pillows that matched the couch. Suddenly Lucy hated the pillows. She tossed them into the near empty closet and closed the door. Tomorrow was her day off. After she checked on Mary, she'd go into Bozeman and do some shopping.

She needed this apartment to feel a whole lot less like Mary Savage. Now that she had Chase's cell number, it was time for her to make him pay.

Chapter Fourteen

Lucy tapped lightly at Mary's door the next morning. Given how sick the woman had been the evening before, she thought she still might be in bed.

So she was a little surprised when Mary answered the door looking as if she'd already showered and dressed for the day.

"Oh good, you look like you're feeling better," she said.

"Much. Thank you again for yesterday."

"Just glad I could help." She started to turn away.

"Do you ride horses?" Mary asked.

Lucy stopped, taken aback by the question. She'd hoped to get close to Mary, befriend her, gain her trust and then finish this. She'd thought it would take more time. "I used to ride when I was younger."

"Would you like to come out to the ranch sometime, maybe on your day off, and go for ride?"

"I would love to." The moment she said it, she knew how dangerous it could be. Chase might show up. She'd managed not to come face-to-face with him. Even with the changes in her appearance, he could recognize her. They'd been lovers. Soul mates.

He would sense who she was the moment they were in the same room.

"Good," Mary was saying. "Let's plan on it. Just let me know what day you're free. And thank you again for yesterday. I don't know what I would have done without you."

Lucy nodded, still taken aback. "I'm glad I was here." She took a step toward the door, feeling strangely uncomfortable. "Off to work," she said as she walked backward for a few steps, smiling like a fool.

Could this really be going as well as she thought it was? She couldn't believe how far she'd come from that night in Arizona when she'd gone into the river. She had Mary Savage, the woman who'd stolen Chase from her, right where she'd wanted her. So why wasn't she more euphoric about it? Her plan was working. There was no reason to be feeling the way she was, which was almost…guilty.

The thought made her laugh as she crossed the street. Guilt wasn't something she normally felt. She was enjoying herself. Maybe too much. She'd thought it would take longer, and she'd been okay with that.

As she settled into work, she realized that she would have to move up her revenge schedule. She was starting to like Mary and that was dangerous. No way could she go on a horseback ride with her, and not just because she might run into Chase. She couldn't let herself start liking Mary. If she weakened… She told herself that wouldn't happen.

But realizing this was almost over, she felt a start. She hadn't given any thought as to what she would do after she was finished here. Where would she go? What would she do? She'd been so focused on destroying Chase and his cowgirl that she hadn't thought about what to do when it was over.

That thought was nagging at her when she looked up to find Chase standing in front of her counter. Panic made her limbs go weak. He wasn't looking at her, but at the board with the day's specials hanging over her head. Could she duck in the back before he saw her? Let the other barista wait on him?

But Amy was busy with another customer. Lucy knew she couldn't hide out in the back until Chase left. All her fears rushed through her, making her skin itch. She'd come so far. She was so close to finishing this. What would she do when he recognized her?

He'd know what she was up to. He'd tell Mary. All of this would have been for nothing. Mary's father was the marshal. It wouldn't take long before he'd know about what had happened in Texas, about the suspicions that had followed her from town to town and finally to Big Sky, Montana. Once he saw through her disguise, and he would. Just like that and it would be all over. She wanted to scream.

"Good morning," he said, and finally looked at her.

"Morning." She held her breath as she met his blue eyes and gave him an embarrassed gap-toothed smile.

He smiled back, his gaze intent on her, but she realized with a start that she saw no recognition in his face. *It's me*, she wanted to say. *The love of your life.*

Don't tell me you don't see me, don't sense me, don't feel me standing right here in front of you.

"I hope you can help me. I want to buy my girlfriend the kind of coffee she loves, but I forgot what it's called. She lives right across the street. I thought you might know what she orders. It's for Mary Savage."

Girlfriend? "Sorry, I'm new."

"That's all right. It was a shot in the dark anyway. Then I guess I'll take one caramel latte and a plain black coffee please."

She stared at him for a moment in disbelief. She'd been so sure he would know her—instinctively—even the way she looked now. But there was no recognition. *None.*

Fury shook her to her core. They'd made *love.* They had a connection. *How could he not know her?*

"You do have plain black coffee, don't you?" he asked when she didn't speak, didn't move.

She let out a sound that was supposed to be a chuckle and turned her back on him. Her insides trembled, a volcano of emotions bubbling up, ready to blow. She fisted her hands, wanting to launch herself across the counter and rip out his throat.

Instead, she thought of Mary and something much better. Ripping out Mary's heart, the heart he was so desperately trying to win back.

She made the latte and poured him a cup of plain black coffee. He handed her a ten and told her to keep the change.

Thanking him, she smiled at the thought of him

standing over Mary Savage's grave. "You have a nice day now."

"You too," he said as he left.

She watched him go, still shocked and furious that the fool hadn't known her. She promised herself that his nice days were about to end, and very soon.

IT WASN'T UNTIL he was headed across the street to Mary's office that Chase looked back at the woman working in the Lone Peak Perk. What was it about her...? He frowned until it hit him. Her voice. Even with the slight lisp and Southern drawl, the cadence of her voice was enough like Fiona's to give him the creeps.

He shuddered, wondering if he would ever be able to put the Fiona nightmare behind him. Yesterday he'd called Rick, and Patty had answered.

"I'm so sorry about what happened with you and Fiona," she'd said. "I just feel so sorry for her. I know it's no excuse, but she had a really rough childhood. Her mother remarried a man who sexually abused her. When she told her mother, the woman didn't believe her. That had to break her heart."

"Did she have anyone else?"

"No siblings or relatives she could turn to. On top of that, her stepfather had three sons."

He had sworn under his breath "So they could have been abusing her too."

"Or Fiona could have lied about all of it. When her mother, stepfather and the three sons died in a fire, I had to wonder. Fiona could have been behind it. I wouldn't put anything past her, would you?"

"Or she could have lied about the sexual abuse and then been racked with guilt when they all died."

Patty had laughed. "You really do try to see the best in people, and even after the number she pulled on you. You're a good guy, Chase. You take care of yourself."

He didn't feel like a good guy. He'd made so many mistakes. Fiona for one. Mary for another. He couldn't do much about Fiona, but he still had a chance to right things with Mary.

Patty had put Rick on the phone. The news was the same. Fiona's body still hadn't turned up.

"Some fisherman will find her downstream. It will be gruesome. A body that's been in the water that long…"

Chase hadn't wanted to think about it.

Like now, he tried to put it behind him as he neared Mary's office door. He wanted to surprise her with coffee. He just wished the barista had known the kind of coffee she drank. Mary was helping him today with his search for a man with the initials J.M. She understood his need to find his father even though there were days when he didn't. Why couldn't he just let it go? His mother apparently had forgiven the man if not forgotten him.

For all he knew, the man could have moved away by now. Or his mother hadn't used his real initials. Or… He shook off the negative thoughts. He would be spending the day with the woman he loved. Did it really matter if they found his father today?

As Chase came in the front door of her office, Mary saw him look back toward the coffee shop and frown. "Is something wrong?" she asked.

He started as if his thoughts had been miles away. "There's a woman working over there. Lucy?"

"I know her." She took the coffee he handed her. Not her usual, but definitely something she liked.

"She just reminded me of someone I used to know—and not in a good way," he said.

"She just started working at Lone Peak Perk only a week or two ago. Why?"

He shook his head. "Just a feeling I got." He seemed to hesitate. "That dangerous woman, Fiona, who I told you about from Arizona. Lucy doesn't look anything like her, but she reminds me of her for some reason."

Mary shook her head. She really did not want to hear anything more about Fiona. "You do realize how crazy that sounds. I know Lucy. She's really sweet. I like her. I rented one of my apartments to her. I'm sure she's nothing like *your*...Fiona."

"She wasn't *my* Fiona. Look, you've never asked, but I didn't date for a long time after I left. I wasn't interested in anyone else. That wasn't why I left and you know it. If I hadn't been drinking, if I hadn't just picked up my mother's ashes the day of the barbecue at my boss's house..."

Mary stood up. "I don't need to hear this."

"Maybe you do," he said, and raked a hand through his hair as he met her gaze. "It was one drunken night. I regretted it right away. She became...obsessed, manufacturing a relationship that didn't exist. She must have stolen my extra house key and copied it. I came home several times to find her in my apartment. She knew I was in love with someone else. But that seemed to make her even more determined to change my mind." He shook his head. "She wouldn't stop. She tried to move some of her stuff into my apartment. Needless to say it got ugly. The last time I saw her…" He hesitated as if he'd never wanted to tell her the details about Fiona and she didn't want to hear them now.

But before she could stop him, he said, "She tried to kill me."

Mary gasped. "You can't be serious."

"She knew I was leaving. She said she wanted to give me a hug goodbye, but when she started to put her arms around me, I saw the knife she'd pulled from her pocket. I would have gotten to Montana weeks sooner, but she sabotaged my pickup. I had to have a new engine put in it." He shook his head. "What I'm saying is that I wouldn't put anything past her. She supposedly drowned in the Colorado River after driving her car into it. But her body was never found."

Mary couldn't believe what she was hearing.

"Lucy doesn't look anything like her except…" He glanced up at her and must have seen the shock and disbelief in her eyes. Couldn't he tell that she didn't want to know anything more about Fiona?

She shook her head, wished this wasn't making her so upset. He'd said Fiona was obsessed with him? It sounded like he was just as obsessed. "This woman really did a number on you, didn't she?"

He held up both hands in surrender. "Sorry. I thought you should know."

About a woman he'd made love to who was now dead? But certainly not forgotten. Even Lucy reminded him of her even though, as he said, she looked nothing like Fiona? Her heart pounded hard in her chest. She pushed her coffee away, feeling nauseous. "We should get going. I need to come back and work."

He nodded. She could tell that he regretted bringing up the subject. So why had he? She never wanted to hear the name Fiona again. Ever.

"I'm sorry. You're right. Forget I mentioned it. I promise not to say another word about her."

But she saw him steal a look toward the coffee shop as they were leaving. He might not mention Fiona's name again, but he was definitely still thinking about her.

Chapter Fifteen

With Mary's mother's help, Chase had narrowed down their search to three local men—Jack Martin, Jason Morrison and Jonathan Mason. Dana had helped him weed out the ones that she knew were too young, too old or hadn't been around at the time.

His mother had been eighteen when she'd given birth to him. If her lover had been older, say twenty-five or thirty as Chase suspected, then his father would now be in his fifties.

Jack Martin owned a variety of businesses in Big Sky, including the art shop where his wife sold her pottery. A bell tinkled over the door as Mary and Chase entered. A woman passed them holding a large box as if what was inside was breakable. Chase held the door for her, before he and Mary moved deeper in the shop.

The place smelled of mulberry candles, a sickeningly sweet fragrance that Mary had never liked. She tried not to breathe too deeply as they moved past displays of pottery toward the back counter.

Jack had begun helping out at the shop during the busiest time, summer, Mary knew. She spotted his gray head coming out of the back with a large pottery bowl, which he set on an open space on a display table. There was a young woman showing several ladies a set of pottery dishes in an adjoining room, and several visitors were looking at pottery lamps at the front of the shop.

As Mary approached, Jack turned and smiled broadly. "Afternoon, is there something I can help you with?"

Mary knew Jack from chamber of commerce meetings, but it took him a second before he said, "Mary Savage. I'm sorry, I didn't recognize you right away."

"This is my friend Chase Steele." She watched for a reaction. For all they knew, Chase's father could have kept track of his son all these years. But she saw no reaction. "Is there a private area where we could speak with you for a moment?"

Jack frowned, but nodded. "We could step into the back." He glanced around to see if there were customers who needed to be waited on. There didn't appear to be for the moment.

"We won't take much of your time," she promised.

Chase tensed next to her as if to say, if Jack Martin was his father, he'd damned sure take as much of his time as he wanted.

Mary was glad that she'd come along. She knew how important this was, and could feel how nervous Chase had become the moment they stepped into the shop.

In the back it was cool and smelled less like the burning candles. "Did you know a woman named

Muriel Steele?" Chase asked the moment they reached a back storage and work area.

Jack blinked in surprised. "Who?"

"Muriel Steele," Mary said with less accusation. "It would have been close to thirty years ago."

Jack looked taken aback. "You expect me to remember that long ago? Who was this woman?"

"One you had an affair with," Chase said, making her cringe. She'd hoped he would let her handle this since he was too emotionally involved.

"That I would remember," the man snapped. "I was married to Clara thirty years ago. We just celebrated our fortieth anniversary." Jack was shaking his head. "I'm not sure what this is about or what this Muriel woman told you, but I have never cheated on my wife."

Mary believed him. She looked to Chase, whom she could tell wasn't quite as convinced.

"Would you be willing to take a DNA test to prove it?" Chase demanded.

"A DNA test? How would that prove..." Realization crossed his face. "I see." His gaze softened. "I'm sorry young man, but I'm not related to you."

"But you'd take the test," Chase pressed.

Jack grew quiet for a moment, his expression sad. "If it would help you, yes, I would."

Mary saw all the tension leave Chase's body. He looked as if the strain had left him exhausted.

"Thank you," Mary said as she heard more customers coming into the shop. "We won't keep you any longer."

"IT'S NOT HIM," Chase said as he climbed behind the wheel and started the pickup's engine. A floodgate of emotions warred inside him. He wasn't sure what he'd hoped for. That he could find his father that quickly and it would be over? He'd wanted to hate the man. Worse, he'd wanted to punch him. But when realization had struck Jack Martin, Chase had seen the pity in the man's eyes.

"No, it wasn't Jack," she said. "Are you up to visiting the rest of them?"

He pulled off his Stetson and raked a hand through his hair. "I'm not sure I can do this. I thought I could but..." He glanced over at her.

"It's all right."

He shook his head. For a moment, they merely sat there, each lost in their own thoughts. Then Chase smiled over at her. "Could we drive up to Mountain Village and have an early lunch and forget all this for a while? Then I promise to take you back to work. I shouldn't have dragged you into this."

She reached over and placed a hand on his arm. He felt the heat of her fingers through his Western shirt. They warmed him straight to his heart and lower. What he wanted was this woman in his arms, in his bed, in his life. He felt as if he had made so many mistakes and was still making them.

"My stomach is still a little upset. I was really sick last night." He looked at her with concern. "I'm sure it was just some twenty-four-hour flu," she said quickly.

"I hope that's all it was," he said. "I was really careful with our picnic lunch."

"And you didn't get sick, so like I said, probably just a flu bug." He must not have looked convinced. "I was just going to eat some yogurt for lunch. Maybe some other time?"

He studied her for a moment, so filled with love for this woman. "You're the best friend I've ever had."

She laughed at that, and took her hand from his arm.

"Is it any wonder that I haven't been able to stop loving you?" he asked.

Their gazes met across the narrow space between them. He could feel the heat, the chemistry. He reached over and cupped the back of her neck, pulling her into the kiss. He heard her breath catch. His pulse quickened. A shaft of desire cut through him, molten hot.

Mary leaned into him and the kiss. It felt like coming home. Chase had always been a great kisser.

As he drew back, he looked into her eyes as if the kiss had also transported him back to when they were lovers.

"You're just full of surprises today, aren't you," she said, smiling at him as she tried to catch her breath. She loved seeing Chase like this, relaxed, content, happy, a man who knew who he was and what he wanted.

The cowboy who'd left her and Montana had been antsy, filled with a need she couldn't understand. Just like he'd been only minutes ago when they'd gone looking for his father.

He needed to find him. She would help him. And then what?

"You have work to do, and I'm keeping you from it," he said. "We can have lunch another day when you feel better and aren't as busy. I've already taken up too much of your morning."

She shook her head as she met his gaze. "If I didn't have this report due—"

"You don't have to explain. You took off this morning to help me. I appreciate that." His smile filled her with joy as much as his words. "We have a lot of lunches in our future. I hope you know how serious I am about us, about our future. I'll do whatever it takes because I know you, Mary Savage. I know your heart."

She felt her eyes burn with tears at the truth in his words. "Tomorrow. Let's go talk to the other two men tomorrow morning."

"Are you sure?" Chase asked. "I don't like keeping you from your work."

She managed to nod. "I'm sure." Swallowing the lump in her throat, she reached to open her door. If she stayed out here with him a minute longer, she feared what she might say. Worse, what she might do. It would have been too easy to fall into his arms and take up where they'd left off and forget all about the report that was due.

But she climbed out of the pickup, knowing it was too soon. She had to know for sure that Chase wouldn't hurt her again. Her heart couldn't take being broken by him again.

As Chase was leaving, he glanced toward the coffee shop. Was Lucy working? He swung his pickup around and parked in front of Lone Peak Perk. Getting out, he told himself to play it cool. He had to see her again. He had to know. But just the thought that he might be right…

As he walked in, Lucy looked up. Surprise registered in those dark eyes. Nothing like Fiona's big blue ones. Still, he walked to the counter. She looked nervous. "Is it possible to get a cup of coffee in a real cup?" he asked. "Just black."

She looked less nervous, but that too could have been his imagination. He wondered what he'd been thinking. The woman looked nothing like Fiona and yet… She was much skinnier, the gapped two front teeth, the short dark hair, the brown eyes. What was it about her that reminded him of Fiona? Mary was right. He was obsessed with the disturbed, irrational woman.

Lucy picked up a white porcelain coffee cup and took her time filling it with black coffee. "Can I get you anything else?" she said with that slight lisp, slight Southern accent. Nothing like Fiona. She flashed him a smile, clearly flirting.

He grinned. "Maybe later." He took the coffee cup by the handle over to an empty spot near the door. Sitting with his back to her, he took a sip. Coffee was the last thing he wanted right now. But he drank it as quickly as the hot beverage allowed.

Taking advantage of a rush of people coming in for their afternoon caffeine fix, he carefully slipped the now empty cup under his jacket and walked out. He'd expected to be stopped, but neither Lucy or the other barista noticed. When he reached his pickup, he carefully set the cup on the center console and headed to the marshal's office.

He would get Hud to run the prints because he had to know what it was about the woman that turned his stomach, and left him feeling like something evil had come to Big Sky.

Lucy couldn't believe that Chase had come back into the coffee shop. She smiled to herself as she whipped up one of the shop's special coffees for a good-tipping patron. As she finished the drink, she turned expecting to see Chase's strong back at the corner table. To her surprise, he'd left during the rush. He'd certainly finished his coffee quickly enough. She frowned as concern slithered slowly through her.

It took her a moment to realize why the hair was now standing up on the back of her neck. The table where Chase had been sitting. His empty porcelain cup wasn't where he should have left it.

She hurriedly glanced around, thinking he must have brought it back to the counter. Otherwise…

Her heart kicked up to double time. Otherwise… He wouldn't have tossed the cup in the trash and she could see from here that he hadn't put it in the tray with the few other dishes by the door.

Which left only one conclusion.

He'd taken the cup.

Why would he—

The reason struck her hard and fast. *He had recognized her.* Warring emotions washed over her. Of course he'd sensed her behind the disguise. She hadn't been wrong about that. It was that unique chemistry that they shared. But at the same time, fear numbed her, left her dumbstruck. She could hear the patron asking her a question, but nothing was registering.

Chase would go to the marshal, Mary's father, have him run the prints. Once that happened… She told herself that there was time. And, there was Deputy Dillon Ramsey.

"Miss! I need a receipt, please."

Lucy shook her head and smiled. "Sorry," she said to the woman, printed out the receipt and handed it to her. "You have a nice day now."

AFTER HIS INITIAL surprise at seeing the cowboy, Hud waved Chase into a chair across from his desk. As the young man came in, he carefully set a white porcelain coffee cup on the edge of the desk. Hud eyed it, then Chase.

"I need you to run the fingerprints on this cup."

The marshal lifted a brow. "For any particular reason?"

"I really don't want to get into it. I'm hoping I'm wrong."

Hud leaned back in his chair. "That's not enough reason to waste the county's time running fingerprints."

"If I'm right, this person could be a danger to Mary. Isn't that enough?"

Rubbing his jaw, he studied the cowboy. "You do understand that unless this person has fingerprints on file—"

"They'll be on file if I'm right."

Intrigued, Hud sighed and said, "Okay. I'll let you know, but it might take a few days."

A deputy was walking past. Hud called to him as he bagged the cup Chase had brought in. "Dillon, run the fingerprints on this cup when you have a minute. Report back to me."

"WE'RE STILL ON for tonight, right?" Lucy asked when Dillon called. The last thing she wanted him to do was cancel.

"You know it."

"Then I have a small favor," she said. "It's one that only you can grant." She could almost hear the man's chest puff out. "And I'll make it worth your while."

"Really?" He sounded intrigued. She reminded herself that he was only doing this to get back at Mary. The thought did nothing for her disposition, but she kept the contempt out of her voice. She needed his help.

"Really. But then maybe you don't have access to what I need down there at the marshal's office."

"Name it. I have the run of the place."

"I believe Chase Steele might have brought in a cup and asked that fingerprints be run on it?"

Dillon chuckled. "The marshal asked me to do it when I had time and report back to him."

"Have you had time?" she asked, her heart in her throat.

"I like to do whatever the marshal asks right away."

She closed her eyes and tried to breathe. Her prints were on file. Chase must have suspected as much.

"I haven't seen him though to give him the report."

Lucy took a breath and let it out slowly. "Is there any way that the report could get lost?"

He snickered. "Now you've got me curious. Why would you care about prints run on a Fiona Barkley?"

So her prints had come back that quickly? "If that report gets lost, I'd be happy to tell you when I see you. Like I said, I'll make it worth your while."

"Are we talking money?" he asked quietly. "Or something else?"

"Or both," she said, her heart pounding. "I can be quite…creative."

He laughed. "What time shall I pick you up?"

"I have a better idea. Why don't I meet you later tonight after I get off my shift? I know just the spot." She told him how to get to the secluded area up in the mountains. She'd spent her free time checking out places for when it came time to end this little charade.

Dillon thought he was going to get lucky—and use her to bring Mary into line. She'd known men like him. He would blackmail her into the next century if she let him.

"I have to work late. Is midnight too late for you?" she asked sweetly.

"Midnight is perfect. I can't wait."

"Me either." The deputy had no idea that he'd walked right into her plot, and now he had a leading role.

Chapter Sixteen

Later that night, as Lucy prepared for her date with Dillon, she couldn't help being excited. She'd spent too much time waiting around, not rushing her plan, being patient and pretending to be someone she wasn't.

Tonight she could let Fiona out. The thought made her laugh. Wait until Dillon met her.

She had to work only until ten, but she needed time to prepare. She knew all about forensics. While she had little faith in the local law being able to solve its way out of a paper bag, she wasn't taking any chances. Amy, who worked at the coffee shop, had seen her talking to Dillon when he'd asked her out, but as far as the other barista knew, he was just another customer visiting after buying a coffee.

If Amy had heard anything, she would have thought he had been asking her for directions. There was no law in him flirting with her, Lucy thought with a grin. That exchange would be the only connection she had to Dillon Ramsey.

At least as far as anyone knew.

She didn't drive to the meeting spot. Instead, she

came in the back way. It hadn't rained in weeks, but a thunderstorm was predicted for the next morning. Any tire or foot tracks she left would be altered if not destroyed. She had worn an old pair of shoes that would be going into the river tonight. Tucked under her arm was a blanket she'd pulled out of a commercial waste bin earlier today.

The hike itself wasn't long as the crow flew, but the route wound through trees and rocks. The waning moon and all the stars in the heavens did little to light her way. She'd never known such a blackness as there was under the dense pines. That's why she was almost on top of Dillon's pickup before she knew it.

As she approached the driver's-side door, she could hear tinny sounding country music coming from his pickup's stereo. He was drumming on his steering wheel and glancing at his watch. From his expression, she could tell that he was beginning to wonder if he'd been stood up.

When she tapped on his driver's-side window, he jumped. His expression changed from surprise to relief. He motioned for her to go around to the passenger side.

She shook her head and motioned for him to get out of the truck.

He put his window down partway, letting out a nose-wrinkling gust of cheap aftershave and male sweat. "It's warmer in here."

"I'm not going to let you get cold."

Dillon gave that a moment's thought before he whirred up the window, killed the engine and music, and climbed out.

Lucy had considered the best way to do this. He had his motivation for asking her out. She had hers for being here. Everyone knew about Dillon and Chase's fight. The two couldn't stand each other. So whom would the marshal's first suspect be if anything happened to Dillon?

She tossed down the blanket she'd brought onto the bed of dried pine needles. Dillon reached for her. He would be a poor lover, one who rushed. "Not yet, baby," she said, holding him at arm's length. "Why don't you strip down, have a seat and let me get ready for you. Turn your back. I want this to be a surprise."

It was like leading a bull to the slaughterhouse.

"Well hurry, because it's cold out tonight," he said as he began to undress. She'd brought her own knife, but when she'd seen his sticking out of his boot, she'd changed her plans.

The moment he sat down, his back to her, she came up behind him, grabbed a handful of his hair and his knife, and slit his throat from ear to ear. It happened so fast that he didn't put up a fight. He gurgled, his hand going to his throat before falling to one side.

She stared down at him, hoping he'd done what he promised and lost the report on her fingerprints. Her only regret was that she hadn't gotten to see the surprise and realization on his smug face. He'd gotten what was coming to him, but she doubted he would have seen it that way.

As she wiped her prints from the knife and stepped away, she kicked pine needles onto her tracks until she was in the woods and headed for the small creek she'd had to cross to get there. She washed her hands, rinsing away his blood. She'd worn a short-sleeved shirt, and with his back to her, she hadn't gotten any of his blood on anything but her hands and wrists.

She scrubbed though, up to her elbows, the ice-cold water making her hands ache. She let them air-dry as she walked the rest of the way back to her vehicle. Once she got rid of the shoes she had on, no one would be able to put her at the murder scene.

THE MOMENT MARY saw her father's face, she knew something horrible had happened. Was it her mother? One of her brothers or someone else in the family? Chase? She rose behind her desk as her father came into her office, his Stetson in hand, his marshal face on.

"Tell me," she said on a ragged breath, her chest aching with dread. She'd seen this look before. She knew when her father had bad news to impart.

"It's Dillon Ramsey."

She frowned, thinking she'd heard him wrong. "Dillon?"

"You weren't with him last night, were you?"

"No, why?"

"He was found dead this morning."

Her first thought was a car accident. The Gallatin Canyon two-lane highway was one of the most dangerous highways in the state with all its traffic and curves through the canyon along the river.

"He was found murdered next to his truck up by Goose Creek."

She stared at him, trying to make sense of this. "How?"

He hesitated but only a moment, as if he knew the details would get out soon enough and he wanted to be the one to tell her. "He was naked, lying on a blanket as if he'd been with someone before that. His throat had been cut."

Her stomach roiled. "Why would someone want to kill him?"

"That's what I'm trying to find out. I'm looking for a friend of his, Grady Birch. Do you know him?"

Mary shook her head. "I never met any of his friends."

Her father scratched the back of his neck for a moment. "I understand that Dillon and Chase got into a confrontation that turned physical."

"Chase? You can't think that Chase… You're wrong. Chase didn't trust him, but then neither did you."

"With good reason as it turns out. I believe that Dillon was involved in the cattle rustling along with his friend Grady Birch."

Mary had to sit back down. All of this was making her sick to her stomach. "I'd broken up with him. I had no plans to see him again. He'd threatened to ask out one of my tenants." She shook her head. "But Chase had nothing to do with this."

The marshal started for the door. "I just wanted you to hear about it from me rather than the Canyon grapevine."

She nodded and watched him leave. Dillon was dead. Murdered. She shuddered.

GRADY BIRCH'S BODY washed up on the rocks near Beckman's Flat later that morning. It was found by a fisherman. The body had been in the water for at least a few days. Even though the Gallatin River never got what anyone would call warm, it had been warm enough to do damage over that length of time.

Hud rubbed the back of his neck as he watched the coroner put the second body that day into a body bag. Dillon was dead; Grady had been dead even longer. What was going on?

He would have sworn that it was just the two of them in on the cattle rustling. But maybe there was someone else who didn't want to share the haul. He'd send a tech crew out to the cabin to see what prints they came up with. But something felt all wrong about this. Killers, he'd found, tended to stay with the same method and not improvise. A drowning was much different from cutting a person's throat. The drowning had been made to look like an accident. But Grady's body had been held down with rocks.

"I'll stop by later," he told the coroner as he walked to his patrol SUV. There was someone he needed to talk to.

Hud found Chase fixing fences on the Sherman Jensen ranch. He could understand why Sherman needed the help and why Chase had agreed to working for board. He was a good worker and Sherman's son was not.

Chase looked up as Hud drove in. He put down

the tool he'd been using to stretch the barbed wire and took off his gloves as he walked over to the patrol SUV.

"Did you get the prints off the cup back?" Chase asked.

Hud shook his head. He'd been a little busy, but he'd check on them the first chance he got. He studied the man his daughter had been in love with as far back as he could remember. Out here in his element, Chase looked strong and capable. Hud had thought of him as a boy for so long. At twenty-four, he'd still been green behind the years. He could see something he hadn't noticed when he saw him at the marshal's office. Chase had grown into a man.

Still he found himself taking the man's measure.

"Marshal," Chase said. "If you've come out here to ask me what my intentions are toward your daughter…" He grinned.

"As a matter of fact, I would like to know, even though that's not why I'm here."

Chase pushed back his Stetson. "I'm going to marry her. With your permission, of course."

Hud chuckled. "Of course. Well, that's good to hear, as far as intentions go, but I'm here on another matter. When was the last time you saw Dillon Ramsey?"

Chase grimaced. "Did he think that's why I was in your office the other day?" He shook his head. "That I'd come there to report our fight? So he decided to tell you his side of it?"

"Actually no. But I heard about it. Heard that if Mary hadn't broken it up, it could have gotten lethal."

"Only because Dillon was going for a knife he had in his boot," Chase said.

Hud nodded. Chase had known about the man's knife. The knife Dillon had been killed with. "So the trouble between you was left unfinished." Chase didn't deny it. "That's the last time you saw him?"

Chase nodded and frowned. "Why? What did he say? I saw the way he was trying to intimidate Mary."

"Not much. Someone cut his throat last night." He saw the cowboy's shocked expression.

"What the hell?"

"Exactly. Where were you last night?"

"Here on the ranch."

"Can anyone verify that you were here the whole time?"

"You can't really believe that I—"

"Can anyone verify where you were?" Hud asked again.

Chase shook his head. "Can't you track my cell phone or something? Better yet, you know me. If I saw Dillon again, I might get in the first punch because I knew he'd fight dirty. But use a knife?" He shook his head. "Not me. That would be Dillon."

Hud tended to believe him. But he also knew about the knife Dillon kept in his boot, and he hadn't seen Chase in years. People change. "You aren't planning to leave town, are you?"

Chase groaned. "I have a carpenter job in Paradise Valley. I was leaving tomorrow to go to work. But I can give you the name of my employer. I really don't want to pass up this job."

Hud studied him for a moment. "Call me with your employer's name. I don't have to warn you not to take off, right?"

Chase smiled. "I'm not going anywhere. Like I told you, I'm marrying your daughter and staying right here."

Hud couldn't help but smile. "Does Mary know that?"

The cowboy laughed. "She knows. That doesn't mean she's said yes yet."

"ARE YOU ALL RIGHT? I just heard the news about the deputy," Chase asked when he called Mary after her father left. "I'm so sorry."

"Dillon and I had broken up, but I still can't believe it. Who would want to kill him?"

"Your father thought I might," he said. "I just had a visit from him."

"What? You can't be serious."

"He'd heard about the fight Dillon and I had in front of your building," Chase said. "I thought maybe you'd mentioned it to him."

"I didn't tell him, but he can't believe that you'd kill anyone."

Chase said nothing for a moment. "The word around town according to Beth Anne is that Dillon had been with someone in the woods. A woman. You have any idea who?"

She thought of Lucy, but quickly pushed the idea away. Dillon had said he was going to ask her out, but she doubted he'd even had time to do that—if he'd been serious. Clearly, he'd been seeing some-one else while he was seeing her.

"I'll understand if you don't want to go with me late to see the next man on my list," Chase said.

"No, I'm going. I'm having trouble getting any work done. I'm still in shock. I know how much find-ing your father means to you. Pick me up?"

"You know it. I'm going to get cleaned up. Give me thirty minutes."

"You questioned Chase about Dillon's murder?" Mary cried when he father answered the phone.

He made an impatient sound. "I'm the marshal, and I'm investigating everyone with a grudge against Dillon Ramsey."

"Chase doesn't hold grudges," she said indig-nantly, making Hud laugh.

"He's a man, and the woman he's in love with was seeing another man who is now dead. Also, he was in an altercation with the dead man less that forty-eight hours ago."

"How did you know about the fi—"

"I got an anonymous call."

"I didn't think anyone but me…" She thought of Lucy. No, Lucy wouldn't do that. Someone else in the area that night must have witnessed it.

"You can't possibly think that Chase would…" She shook her head adamantly. "It wasn't Chase."

"Actually, I think you're right," her father said. "I just got the coroner's report. The killer was right-handed. I noticed Chase is left-handed."

Mary felt herself relax. Not that she'd ever let herself think Chase was capable of murder, but she'd been scared that he would be a suspect because of their altercation.

As she looked up, she saw Lucy on her way to work. The woman turned as if sensing she was being watched, and waved before coming back to the front door of the office to stick her head in.

"Mary, are you all right? I just heard the news on the radio about that deputy you were seeing, the one your cowboy got into a fight with the other night."

"I know, it's terrible, isn't it?"

"You don't think Chase—"

"No." She shook her head. "My dad already talked to him. It wasn't him."

Lucy lifted a brow. "Chase sure was angry the other night."

"Yes, but the forensics proved that Chase couldn't have done it." Mary waved a hand through the air as if she couldn't talk about it, which she couldn't. "Not that I ever thought Chase could kill someone."

Lucy still didn't look convinced. "I think everyone is capable. It just has to be the right circumstances."

"You mean the wrong ones," Mary said, the conversation making her uncomfortable. She no longer wanted to think about how Dillon had died or who might have killed him.

"Yes," Lucy said, and laughed.

"Did you ever go out with Dillon?" Mary asked, and wished she hadn't at Lucy's expression.

"Seriously?" The woman laughed. "Definitely not my type. Why would you ask me that?"

"He mentioned that he might ask you out. I thought maybe—"

Lucy sighed. "Clearly, he was just trying to make you jealous. I think he came into the coffee shop once that I can remember. You really thought I was the woman who had sex with him in the woods?"

"We don't know that's what happened."

"It's what everyone in town is saying. They all think that the killer followed the deputy out to the spot where he was meeting some woman. That's why I asked about Chase. If your cowboy thought it was you on that blanket with him…"

"That's ridiculous. Anyway, it wasn't me."

"But maybe in the dark, Chase didn't know that."

"Seriously, Lucy, you don't know him. I do. Chase wouldn't hurt anyone."

"Sorry. Not something you want to dwell on at this time of the morning. I can't believe you thought I could be the woman with him."

And yet Lucy seemed determine to believe that Chase had been the killer.

"Coming over for your coffee?" Lucy asked. "I can have it ready for you as soon as I get in."

"No, actually. I have an errand to run this morning."

Lucy frowned but then brightened. "Well, have a nice day. Maybe I'll see you later."

From the window, Mary saw her hesitate as if she wanted to talk longer before she closed the door and started across the street. She seemed to quicken her pace as Chase drove up.

Mary hurried out, locking her office door behind

her before climbing into his pickup. He smiled over at her. "You okay? I saw Lucy talking to you as I drove up."

"Nothing important."

"Then let's get it over with. I never realized how… draining this could be," Chase said.

"Who's next?"

"Jason Morrison."

Morrison was a local attorney. His office was only a few doors down from Mary's. They'd called to make an appointment and were shown in a little before time.

Jason was tall and slim with an athletic build. He spent a lot of time on the slopes or mountain biking, and had stayed in good shape at fifty-five. He was a nice looking man with salt and pepper dark hair and blue eyes. When his secretary called back to say that his eleven o'clock was waiting, he said to send them on back.

Jason stood as they entered and came around his desk to shake Mary's hand and then Chase's.

Mary watched as he shook Chase's hand a little too long, his gaze locked on the younger man's.

Was it Chase's blue eyes, or did Jason see something in him he recognized?

"Please, have a seat," the attorney said, going behind his desk and sitting down. "What can I do for the two of you?"

"We're inquiring about a woman named Muriel Steele," Mary said. "We thought you might have known her twenty-seven years ago."

Jason leaned back in his chair and looked from

Mary to Chase and back. "Muriel. Has it been that long ago?" He shook his head. "Yes, I knew her." He frowned. "Why are you asking?"

"I'm her son," Chase said.

Jason's gaze swung back to him. "I thought there was something about you that was familiar when we shook hands. Maybe it's the eyes. Your mother had the most lovely blue eyes."

As Chase started to rise, Mary put a hand on his thigh to keep him in his chair. "Chase is looking for his father."

"His father?" He glanced at Mary and back to Chase.

"When my mother left Big Sky, she was pregnant with me, but I suspect you already know that," Chase said through clenched teeth.

The attorney looked alarmed. "I had no idea. Wait a minute. You think I was the one who…" He held up his hands. "I knew your mother, but I was already married by then. Linda was pregnant with our daughter Becky." He was shaking his head.

"My mother left a diary," Chase said.

Jason went still. "If she said it was me…" He shook his head. "I'm sorry, but I'm not your father."

"She didn't name her married lover," Chase said. "Just his initials. J.M. Quite a coincidence you knew her and you have the exact initials."

A strange look crossed the man's face. "I'm sorry. Like I said, you have the wrong man."

"Then you wouldn't mind submitting to a DNA test," Mary said.

"I'm a lawyer. No good can come of submitting

to a DNA test, not with the legal system like it is. No offense to your father the marshal, ma'am," he added quickly.

"So you're saying no?" Chase asked as he got to his feet.

Jason sighed. "I want to help you, all right? If it comes to that, I'd get a DNA test. I assume there are others you're talking to?"

"Actually, a friend of yours," Mary said. "Jonathan Mason."

Jason groaned. He looked as if he wanted to say more, but changed his mind. "My heart goes out to you. But maybe there was a reason your mother never told you who your father was."

"Other than she wanted to protect him?" Chase demanded.

Jason sighed again. "I wish I could help you. I really do. But after all this time…"

"You think I should let it go?" Chase leaned toward the man threateningly.

Jason held up his hands. "I can see your frustration."

"It's not frustration. It's anger. The man knocked up my mother, broke her heart and her spirit, and let her raise me alone. She was only seventeen when she became pregnant, had no education and no way to support herself but menial jobs. So, I'm furious with this man who fathered me."

"Then why find him? What good will it do?" the lawyer asked.

Chase leaned back some. "Because I want to look him in the eye and tell him what I think of him."

Mary rose and so did the attorney. "We'll probably be back about that DNA test," she said.

Jason nodded, but he didn't look happy about it. His gaze went to Chase and softened. "I cared about your mother, but I wasn't her lover."

"I guess we'll see," Chase said as they left.

"It's him," Chase said as they left the attorney's office. His heart was pounding. He thought about what the man had said. "It's him, I'm telling you."

"I don't know."

"He admitted knowing her. You saw the way he looked at me. He knew the moment he shook my hand. He practically admitted it."

"But he didn't admit it," Mary pointed out.

"He's a lawyer. He's too smart to admit anything."

"He admitted that he knew her, that he cared about her. Chase, I think he's telling the truth."

He stopped walking to sigh deeply. Taking off his Stetson, he raked a hand through his hair and tried to calm down. "I don't know why I'm putting myself through this. I'm twenty-eight years old. He's right. What do I hope to get out of this?"

"A father."

He let out a bark of a laugh. "That ship has sailed. I don't need a father."

"We all need family."

He shook his head. "When I find him, I want to tell him off—not bond with him. Hell, I want to punch him in his face."

At a sound behind them, they turned to see Jason hurrying toward his car.

"I think we should follow him," Mary said as they watched him speed away.

Chase nodded, his gaze and attention on the attorney. "I think you're right. He certainly took off fast enough right after we talked to him. Let's go."

They climbed into his pickup, turned around in the middle of the street and followed at a distance. "Where do you think he's going?"

"Good question. Maybe home to talk to his wife."

Mary shook her head. "He doesn't live in this direction."

"What if he is going to warn Jonathan Mason?"

"Maybe. But only if Jonathan is up at the mountain resort." Chase drove up the road toward Lone Peak.

"Maybe he's going to lunch," he suggested.

"Maybe." After a few miles, the lawyer turned into the Alpine Bar parking lot.

Jason parked, leaped out and went inside.

"He could have called someone to meet him," Chase said.

She nodded. "Let's give him a minute and go inside."

Chase pulled into the lot next to the attorney's car. It was early so there were only three cars out front. During ski season, the place would have been packed. "Recognize any of the rigs?"

She shook her head.

"Have I thanked you for doing this for me? I really do appreciate it."

She smiled over at him. "You have thanked me. I'm glad to help, you know that. But Chase—"

"I know. Try not to lose my temper."

"I don't want to have to bail you out of jail," she said, still smiling.

"But you would, wouldn't you?" He reached out and stroked her cheek, his gaze locking with hers. "I've never loved you more than I do right now, Mary Cardwell Savage." He drew back his hand. "Marry me when this is all over."

She laughed and shook her head.

"I'm serious. What is it going to take to make you realize that you're crazy about me? I want to make you Mrs. Chase Steele. We can have the big wedding I know your mother wants. But I was thinking—"

"You're stalling. Come on, let's go in," she said, and they climbed out. He caught up with her and, taking her arm, pulled her around to face him.

"For the record? I was serious about asking you to marry me. Soon." As he pushed open the door, country music from the jukebox spilled out. Chase heard a familiar song, and wished he and Mary were there to dance—not track down his no-count biological father.

He spotted Jason at the bar talking to the bartender, a gray-haired man with wire-rimmed glasses. As the door closed behind them, a man came through the back door. He caught a glimpse of a residence through the doorway and a ramp before the door closed.

The man motioned to Jason to join him at one of the tables in the back.

"Do you recognize him?" he asked Mary.

"It's Jim Harris," Mary said, and grabbed Chase's

arm to stop him. "What if the initials J.M. were short for Jim? Jim Harris owns this bar. He and his wife live in a house behind it."

Chase stared at the man the attorney had joined. Blond, blue-eyed, midfifties. The scary part was that as he watched the man, he saw himself in Jim Harris's expression, in the line of his nose, the way he stroked his jaw as he listened.

Chase didn't know that he'd stopped in the middle of the room and was still staring until the man looked up. Their gazes met across the expanse of the bar.

Jim Harris froze.

Chapter Seventeen

Chase felt as if he'd been punched in the stomach. He couldn't breathe, had no idea how he'd gotten out of the bar. He found himself standing outside, bent over, gasping for breath, Mary at his side.

The bar door opened behind him. Sucking in as much air as he could, he straightened and turned. He was a good two inches taller than his father, but the similarities were all too apparent. He stared at the man who was staring just as intensely back at him.

"I didn't know," Jim said, his voice breaking. "I had no idea."

"You didn't know my mother was pregnant? Or you didn't know you had a son?" Chase demanded, surprised he could speak.

"Neither." The man suddenly dropped to the front steps of the bar and put his head in his hands. "When Jason told me…" He lifted his head. "I didn't believe him until I saw you."

"How was it you didn't know?" Mary asked. For a moment, Chase had forgotten she was there.

"She never told me…" Jim moaned.

"You weren't at all curious why she left?" Chase

said, his voice breaking. His strength was coming back. So was his anger.

"I knew why Muriel left," the man said, meeting his gaze. "I separated from my wife when I met your mother. We fell in love. I was in the process of filing for divorce to marry Muriel when…" His voice broke and he looked away. "My wife was in a car accident. She almost died."

"And you decided not to leave her," Chase said, nodding as if he could feel his mother's pain. She'd been young and foolish, fallen for a man who was taken only to realize all his promises had come to nothing—and she was pregnant with his child. So she hadn't told him. What would have been the point since by then she knew he was staying with his wife?

The door behind Jim opened. Chase heard a creak and looked up to see a woman in a wheelchair framed in the doorway. The woman had graying hair that hung limp around her face. She stared at him for a long moment before she wheeled back and let the door close behind her. He looked at his father, who was looking at him.

"She's been in a wheelchair since the accident," Jim said quietly as he got to his feet. "I blamed myself since she had her accident after an argument we had over the bar. The bar," he said with disgust. "We both wanted the divorce. That wasn't the problem. It was the bar. I wanted to keep it. She wanted it sold, and half the money. If only I'd let her have it…" His voice dropped off. "I wanted to be with your mother. Muriel was the love of my life. If I'd known she was pregnant…"

"But she didn't tell you after she heard about your wife's accident," Chase said more to himself than his father.

Jim nodded. "If I'd known where your mother had gone…" He didn't finish because it was clear he didn't know what he would have done.

Chase thought of how close his father had been in the years from fifteen on that he'd lived and worked on the Cardwell Ranch. All that time, his father had been not that far away. But there was no reason for their paths to cross. His father's bar was up on the mountain at the resort and Chase had lived down in the canyon.

He looked at his father and could see that the man had paid the price for all these years, just as his mother had. Jim Harris stood for a moment, his hands hanging at his sides, a broken man. "I'm sorry you didn't find a better father than me." With that he turned and went back inside.

Chase felt Mary touch his arm. "I can drive," she said, and took his pickup keys from his hand.

HOURS LATER, SHE and Chase lay curled up in her apartment bed, his strong arms around her. They'd stayed up and talked until nearly daylight, and finally exhausted had climbed into her bed.

Chase had found his father. Not the man he'd thought he was going to find. Not a man he'd wanted to punch. A man who looked like him. A man who'd made mistakes, especially when it came to love.

Mary had told him what she knew about Jim and his wife, Cheryl. They'd gotten married young when

Cheryl had been pregnant, but she'd lost the baby and couldn't have another. It had been a rocky marriage.

"Jim said they were separated when he met your mother, but they must have kept it quiet. She wandered down in Meadow Village and he lived up on the mountain behind the bar." She'd called her mother to ask her what she knew and Jim and Cheryl.

Dana had said she remembered that Cheryl had been staying with a sister down in Gateway near Bozeman when she'd had her accident.

"So no one knew about my mother and Jim," Chase had said.

"Apparently not. I guess they hadn't wanted it to be an issue in the divorce, especially since the bar was already one."

When it got late and they'd talked the subject nearly to death, she'd suggested they go to bed.

"Mary, I—"

"Not to make love. Sleep. I don't want you leaving after what you've been through. Also, it won't be long before morning. We both need sleep and you have to leave for you carpentry job tomorrow."

Now as they lay in bed, Chase said, "I don't want to be like him, a coward, a man who never followed his heart."

"You're not like him."

He made a groaning sound. "I have been. Out of fear. I should have stayed in Montana and fought for you. Instead, I left. I was miserable the whole time. I missed you and Montana so much. I didn't think I was good enough for you. I'm still not sure I am."

She touched her finger to his lips. "That's ridiculous and all behind us."

"Is it? Because I still feel like you don't trust me," Chase whispered in the dark room as he pulled her closer. "What is it going to take to make you trust me again?"

LUCY LAY IN BED listening to the noises coming from upstairs. She hadn't been able to sleep since she'd heard Mary come in with Chase. They'd gone right upstairs. She had heard them moving around and the low murmur of voices, but she hadn't been able to tell what was going on until minutes ago when they'd gone into the bedroom. It was right over her own.

Not that she could hear what they were doing. The building was solid enough that she'd had to strain to hear anything at all. But she'd heard enough to know that they were still in the bedroom. Both of them. She knew exactly what they were doing, and it was driving her mad.

Getting up, she went into the living room, got herself a stiff drink and sprawled on the couch. She had hoped that Mary wouldn't fall for him again. What was wrong with the woman? How could she trust a man like that? Lucy fumed and consumed another couple of shots until she'd fallen asleep on the couch only to be awakened by movement upstairs later in the morning.

She sat up and listened. Chase's boots on the stairs. Mary's steps right behind him. Lucy listened to them descend the stairs as she fought the urge to charge out into the hall and attack them both with her bare hands. Mary was a fool.

She cracked her door open to listen and heard them talking about Chase leaving the area for a carpenter job he was taking. Leaving? She tiptoed to the top of the stairs, keeping to the shadows. They had stopped on the main floor landing.

"I don't like leaving you," he said. "But I'll be back every weekend. This job will only last about six weeks, and then my boss said we have work around Big Sky so I'll see you every night. That's if you want to see me."

Lucy couldn't hear what Mary said, but she could hear the rustle of clothing. Had Mary stepped into his arms? Were they kissing? She felt her blood boil.

"You'll be careful?" Chase said.

"Please, don't start that again."

Lucy heard the tension in her voice and moved down a few steps so she could hear better.

"I'm sorry, but there is still something about Lucy that bothers me," Chase said. "Doesn't it seem strange that three people have died since she came to town?"

"You can't believe that she had anything to do with that."

"Lucy just walks into the job at the coffee shop after the last new hire gets run down on the road? Then she moves into the same apartment Christy Shores was going to rent before she was murdered? A coincidence?"

"Big Sky is a small place, so not that much of a coincidence since I live across the street from the coffee shop and had an apartment for rent."

"And didn't you tell me that Dillon was going to ask Lucy out?"

She rolled her eyes. "And that was reason enough to kill him? She said he hadn't and she wouldn't have gone out with him if he had."

Chase shrugged. "It's…creepy."

"What's creepy is that she reminds you of an old girlfriend."

"Fiona wasn't my girlfriend. But Lucy definitely reminds me of her. Fiona went after what she wanted at all costs and the consequences be damned."

"I really don't want to talk about this."

"I just want you to be careful, that's all. Don't put so much trust in her. Promise?"

"I promise. I don't want to argue with you right before you leave me."

Lucy could hear the two of them smooching again.

"I'll be back Friday night. I'd love to take you to dinner."

"I'd love that."

Lucy pressed herself against the wall as the door opened and light raced up the stairs toward her. She stayed where she was and tried to catch her breath. Chase suspected she was Fiona. So far he hadn't convinced Mary. Nor had the marshal gotten her prints off the cup and found out she was Fiona Barkley. The deputy had done his job. She almost felt bad about killing him.

But it was only a matter of time before Mary started getting suspicious.

After hearing her go into her office, Lucy inched her way back to her apartment. She wanted to scream, to destroy the apartment, anything to rid herself of the fury boiling up inside her. She'd tried to be patient, but the more she was around Mary, the more she hated seeing her with Chase.

She clenched her fists. Mary had said she wasn't sure about the two of them. Liar. But Lucy knew Chase was to blame. He'd somehow tricked his way into Mary's bed. Chase was the one chasing the cowgirl.

She'd come here planning to kill them both. It wasn't Mary's fault that Chase went around breaking women's hearts. But even as she thought it, she knew that Mary had disappointed her by falling for Chase all over again.

Not that it mattered, she thought as she calmly walked into the kitchen, opened the top drawer and took out the knife she'd planned to use on the deputy. She stared at it, telling herself it was time to end this and move on. And there was only one way to finish it.

"It's my day off," Lucy announced as she came out of her apartment as Mary was headed downstairs a few days later.

Mary couldn't help but look confused as she took in Lucy's Western attire and tried to make sense of the words. She knew that she'd been avoiding her tenant since their conversation about Dillon and Chase and felt guilty for it.

"Oh no, I'm sorry," Lucy said quickly. "You forgot. That's all right." She started to turn back toward her apartment.

"Horseback riding." Mary racked her brain, trying to remember if they'd made a definite date to go.

"You said on my day off. I thought I'd mentioned that I would be off today. Don't worry about it. I'm sure we can go some other time."

"No," Mary said quickly. "I did forget, but it will only take me a moment to change." She was thinking about what work she'd promised to do today, but she could get it done this afternoon or even work late if she had to. She didn't want to disappoint Lucy. The woman had looked so excited when she'd first mentioned it.

The more Chase had said Lucy reminded him of the woman he'd known in Arizona, the more Mary had defended her. If she never heard the name Fiona again, she'd be ecstatic.

And yet she found herself pulling away from Lucy, questioning the small things, like how close they'd become so quickly. Also she'd always tried to keep tenants as just that and not friends. More than anything, it was Chase's concern that had her trying to put distance between her and Lucy. Mary didn't want the woman always reminding him of Fiona.

So the last thing she wanted to do today was go horseback riding with the woman. But it had been her idea, and she had invited her. If anything, she prided herself on keeping her word. After this though, she would put more distance between them.

"I'll run across the street and get us some coffee," Lucy said, all smiles. "I'm so excited. It's been so long since I've been on a horse."

Mary hurried back upstairs to change. She missed

Chase. He called every night and they talked for hours. He never mentioned his father, and she didn't bring it up. But she'd felt a change in him since discovering that Jim Harris was his biological father. He seemed stronger, more confident, more sure of what he wanted. He said he didn't want to be like the man. She wasn't sure exactly what he'd meant. Jim Harris was an unhappy man who'd made bad decisions before finding himself between a rock and hard place. She wondered if Chase could ever forgive him. Or if he already had.

When she came back downstairs, dressed for horseback riding, she found Lucy sitting at her desk. Two coffees sat on the edge away from the paperwork. Mary stopped in the doorway and watched for a moment as Lucy glanced through the papers on her desk before taking the card with the daisies that Chase had sent her, reading it and putting it back. As she did, she caught one of the daisies in her fingers.

Mary watched her crush it in her hand before dropping it into the trash can. She felt a fissure of irritation that the woman had been so nosy as to read the card let alone destroy one of the daisies. It was clear that Lucy resented Chase. Was she jealous? Did she not want Mary to have any other relationships in her life?

She cleared her voice, and Lucy got up from her desk quickly.

"Sorry, I was just resting for a moment." Lucy flashed her a gap-toothed smile. "I'm on my feet all day. It will be nice to sit on the back of a horse for a while."

HUD HAD THREE unsolved murders within weeks of each other and no clues. He got up to get himself some coffee when he remembered the cup Chase had brought in to be fingerprinted.

With a curse, he recalled that he'd given the cup to Dillon. Back in his office, he called down to the lab. "Last week a cup was brought down to be fingerprinted. I haven't seen the results yet."

The lab tech asked him to hold for a moment. "I have the order right here. I did the test myself, but I don't see my report on file. You didn't get a copy?"

"No, who did you give it to?"

"Dillon Ramsey, the deputy who brought it down. He asked that I give it to him personally. I did."

Hud swore. "You don't happen to remember—"

"The prints *were* on file," the tech said. Just as Chase had thought they would be. "Give me a minute. It was an unusual name. Fiona. Fiona Barkley."

Hud wrote it down and quickly went online. Fiona Barkley had been fingerprinted several times when questioned by police, starting with a house fire when she was eleven. Her entire family died in the fire.

The marshal shook his head as he saw that she'd been questioned and fingerprinted in a half dozen other incidents involving males that she'd dated.

Where had Chase gotten this cup? He put in a call to the cowboy's number. It went straight to voice mail. He didn't leave a message. Mary had said that Chase would be home Friday night. Hud would ask him then.

AS CHASE TOOK a break, he noticed that Rick had left several messages for him to call. Tired from a long day, he almost didn't call him back. He wasn't sure he could stay awake long enough to talk to both Mary and Rick, and he much preferred to talk to Mary before he fell asleep. But the last message Rick had left said it was important.

Chase figured that Fiona's body had been found, and Rick wanted him to know. So why hadn't he just left that message? The phone rang three times before Rick answered. Chase could hear a party going on in the background and almost hung up.

"Chase, I'm so glad you called back. Hold on." He waited and a few moments later, Rick came back on, the background noise much lower. "Hey, I hate to call you with bad news."

"They found her body?"

"Ah, no. Just the opposite. Some dentist down on the border recognized Fiona's photograph from a story in the newspaper about her disappearance. He contacted authorities. Chase, it looks like Fiona is alive. Not just that. She had the dentist change her appearance. Apparently, the Mexican dentist thought it was strange since she'd obviously been in some kind of accident. But he gave her a gap between her two front teeth."

Chase felt his heart stop dead. Lucy. The woman living on the floor below Mary. Lucy. The barista who Mary had befriended. He tried to take a breathe, his mind racing. Hadn't he known? He'd sensed it gut deep, as if the woman radiated evil. Why hadn't he listened to his intuition?

"I have to go." He disconnected and quickly dialed Mary's cell phone number. It went straight to voice mail. "When you get this, call me at once. It's urgent. Don't go near Lucy. I'll explain when I see you. I'm on my way to Big Sky now." He hung up and called the ranch. Mary's mother answered.

"Dana, it's Chase. Have you seen Mary?"

"No. Chase, what's wrong?"

"I'm on my way there. If you see or hear from Mary, keep her there. Don't let her near Lucy, the barista at Lone Peak Perk, okay? Tell Hud. She's not who she is pretending to be. She's come to Montana to hurt me. I'm terrified that she will hurt Mary." He hung up and ran out to his pickup. He could be home within the hour. But would that be soon enough?

Or was it already too late?

Chapter Eighteen

"You haven't touched your coffee," Lucy said, glancing over at her as Mary drove her pickup to the ranch. Lucy had wanted to see the place and asked if they could take the back roads—unless Mary was in a hurry.

She'd taken a sip of the coffee. It had tasted bitter. Or maybe the bitter taste in her mouth had nothing to do with the coffee and more to do with what she'd seen earlier in her office—Lucy going through her things.

Now she took another sip. It wasn't just bitter. It had a distinct chalky taste—one that she remembered only too well. Even as she thought it, though, she was arguing that she was only imagining it. Otherwise, it would mean that there'd been something in the coffee that Lucy had brought her that day that had made her deathly ill—and again today.

"My stomach is a little upset," she said, putting the coffee cup back into the pickup's beverage holder.

Lucy looked away, her feelings obviously hurt. "Maybe we should do this some other day. I feel like you're not really into it."

"No, I asked you and this is the first day you've had off," Mary said, hating that she'd apparently forgotten. Worse, hating that she'd let Chase's suspicions about Lucy get to her. Not that the woman hadn't raised more suspicions by her actions earlier.

Lucy turned away as if watching the scenery out the window. Mary pretended to take a sip of her coffee, telling herself that after today, she would distance herself from the woman and the coffee shop—at least for a while. It wasn't good to get too involved with a tenant, maybe especially this one.

Even the little bit of the coffee on the tip of her tongue had that chalky taste and made her want to gag. She looked over at Lucy as she settled her cup back into the pickup's beverage holder. She'd taken the long way to the ranch for Lucy but now she regretted it, just wanting to get this trip over with.

As she slowed for a gate blocking the road, she asked, "Lucy, would you mind getting the gate?"

Without a word, the woman climbed out as soon as Mary stopped the vehicle. Easing open her door, Mary poured half of the coffee onto the ground and quietly closed her door again. Lucy pushed the gate back and stepped aside as Mary drove through and then waited for her to close it.

Would she notice the spot on the ground where the coffee had been dumped? She hoped not. She also hoped that she was wrong about the chalky taste and what might have caused it. She didn't want to be wrong about Lucy, she thought as she watched the young woman close the gate and climb back in the truck.

Mary saw her glance at the half-empty coffee cup. Did she believe that Mary had drunk it?

Looking away again, Lucy asked, "How much farther to where you keep the horses?"

"Just over the next hill." Mary had called ahead and asked one of the wranglers to saddle up her horse and a gentle one for Lucy. As they topped the hill, she could see two horses waiting for them tied up next to the barn. She tried to breathe a sigh of relief. Maybe Lucy had gotten up on the wrong side of the bed this morning. Or maybe she had drugged Mary's coffee and was angry that she hadn't drunk it.

"Is everything all right?" Lucy asked. "You seem upset with me."

Mary shot her a look. "I'm sorry. I just feel bad that I forgot about our horseback ride today. That's all."

"Not just your upset stomach?" the woman asked pointedly.

"That too, but I'm feeling better. There is no place I like better than the back of a horse."

Lucy said no more as Mary parked behind the bar and they got out. She helped the woman into the saddle. After she swung up onto her mount, they headed off on a trail that would take them to the top of the mountain. Mary was already planning on cutting the horseback ride short as she led the way up the trail.

"I'm out of sorts this morning too," Lucy said behind her. "I haven't slept well worrying about you."

Mary turned in her saddle to look back at her. "Worrying about *me*?"

"I probably shouldn't say anything, but there is something about Chase that bothers me."

She wanted to laugh out loud. Or at least say, *There's something about you that bothers him.* Instead, she said, "There is nothing to worry about."

"You just seem to be falling back into his arms so quickly. I heard him up in your apartment. He didn't leave until the next morning."

Mary felt a sliver of anger ripple through her. Chase was right about one thing. Lucy had become too involved in her life. "Lucy, that is none of your business."

"I'm sorry, I thought we were friends. You told me that night in my apartment all about him and the deputy."

"Yes." That, she saw now had been a mistake. "Then you know I never stopped loving him."

"But he stopped loving you."

She brought her horse up short as the trail widened, and Lucy rode up beside her. "Lucy—"

"You're the one who told me about this Fiona woman he had the affair with," she said, cutting Mary off.

"It was *one* night."

Lucy shrugged. "Or so he says. You said this woman called you. Said they were engaged. Why would she do that if they'd only had one date?"

Had Mary told her about that? She couldn't remember.

Lucy must have seen the steam coming out of her ears. "Don't get angry. I'm only saying this because you need someone who doesn't have a dog in the fight to tell you the truth."

She had to bite her tongue not to say that they didn't have that kind of friendship. "I appreciate your concern. But I know what I'm doing."

"It's just that he hurt you. I don't want to see him do it again."

"We probably shouldn't talk about this," Mary said, and spurred her horse forward. The sooner they got to the top of the mountain and finished this ride, the better. Chase was right. Somehow Lucy had wormed her way deep into Mary's life. Too deep for the short time they had known each other.

Lucy was jealous of her being with Chase, she realized. Had he sensed that? Is that why he didn't like Lucy? Why she reminded him of Fiona?

They rode in silence as the trail narrowed again, and Lucy was forced to fall in behind her. When they finally reached the top of the mountain, Mary felt as if she could breathe again. She blamed herself. Lucy had been kind to her. Lucy had managed to somehow always be there when needed. Mary had let her get too close, and now it was going to be awkward having her for a tenant directly below her apartment.

She just had to make it clear that her love life was none of Lucy's business. When they rode back to town, she'd talk to her.

HUD LISTENED TO his wife's frantic call. He thought of the cup that Chase had brought him wanting the fingerprints checked. "Lucy? You're sure that's what he said?"

"She's a barista at a coffee shop across the street from Mary's building and one of her tenants." He thought of the plain white cup.

"Chase sounded terrified. He's on his way here. I tried to call Mary before I called you. Her phone went straight to voice mail. I'm scared."

"Okay, don't worry," Hud said. "I'll find this Lucy woman and see what's going on. If you see Mary, call me. Keep her there until I get to the bottom of this."

He disconnected, fear making his heart pound, and headed for his patrol SUV. The town of Big Sky had spread out some since the early days when few would have called it a real town. Still, it didn't take him but a few minutes to get to the coffee shop. As he walked in, he looked about for a barista with the name tag Lucy. There was an Amy and a Faith, but no Lucy.

"Excuse me," he said to the one called Amy. "Is Lucy working today?"

"Day off," she called over her shoulder as she continued to make a coffee that required a lot of noise.

"Do you know where she might have gone?" A headshake. He looked to the other barista. Faith shook her head as well and shrugged.

Dana had said that Lucy rented an apartment across the street. He headed over to Mary's building. With his master key, he opened the door and started up the stairs. An eerie quiet settled over him as he reached the second floor. He knocked at the first door. No answer. He tried the other one. No answer.

He was thinking about busting down the doors

when the second one opened. A young man peered out. "I was looking for Lucy," he said.

"Lucy? The woman who is renting the apartment next door? I haven't met her but I overheard her and Mary talking about going horseback riding."

"Do you know where?"

"On Mary's family ranch, I would assume."

Lucy had gone horseback riding with Mary? He quickly called the ranch as he took the stairs three at a time down to his patrol SUV. "Dana," he said when she answered, "a tenant in the building said that Lucy and Mary went horseback riding. You're sure they aren't there?"

"I don't see her rig parked by the barn unless…" He could hear Dana leaving the house and running toward the barn. "She parked in back. They must have come in the back way," she said, out of breath. "Oh, Hud, they're up in the mountains somewhere alone." He heard the sound of a vehicle come roaring up.

"Who is that?" he demanded.

"Chase."

The marshal swore. "Tell him to wait until I get there. Don't let him go off half-cocked." But even as he said the words, he knew nothing was going to stop Chase. "I'm on my way." The moment he disconnected, he raced toward his patrol SUV.

Hud swore as he climbed behind the wheel, started the engine and headed for the ranch. It didn't take much to put the coffee cup and the barista named Lucy together with an apparently disturbed woman named Fiona Barkley who had a lot of priors in her past. His dead deputy had seen the report and kept the results to himself. He had the tie-in with Dillon and the barista, he thought his stomach roiling. His daughter was on a horseback ride with a killer.

LUCY GRITTED HER teeth as she watched Mary ride to the edge of the mountain and dismount. As she stared at her back, there was nothing more Lucy could say. She could tell that Mary was angry with her. Angry at a friend who was just trying to help her. Mary thought she knew Chase better than her.

Lucy wanted to laugh at that. She knew the cowboy better than Mary assumed. Maybe it was time to enlighten her. Look how easily Chase had cast her aside. How he'd gotten that irritated look whenever he saw her after that first night. He'd wanted her to go away. He'd gotten what he wanted from her and no longer needed her.

Instead, he thought he needed Mary. Sweet, precious Mary. She glared at the woman's back as she rode toward her, reined in and dismounted. She told herself that she'd tried to save Mary. It was Mary's own fault if she wouldn't listen. Now the cowgirl would need to die. It would have to look like an accident. Earlier, she'd thought about pulling the pocketknife she'd brought and jamming it into the side of her horse.

But she'd realized that Mary had been raised on horses. She probably wouldn't get bucked off when the horse reared or even when it galloped down the narrow trail in pain.

No, it had been a chance she couldn't take. But

one way or another Mary wasn't getting off this mountain alive, she thought as she stepped over to stand beside her.

The view was just as Mary had said it was. They stood on a precipice overlooking a dozen mountains that stretched far into the horizon.

Below them was the canyon with its green-tone river snaking through the pines and canyon walls. It would have been so easy to push Mary off and watch her tumble down the mountain. But there was always the chance that the fall wouldn't kill her.

Lucy reached into her pocket and fingered the gun as she said, "I slept with Chase in Arizona."

Chapter Nineteen

Chase roared up in his pickup and leaped out as Dana ran toward him.

"The wrangler had horses saddled for them. He said they headed up the road into the mountains," she told him as he rushed toward her. He could see that she'd been saddling horses. "Hud wants you to wait for him. If this woman is as dangerous as you say she is—"

"I'm the one she wants. Not Mary. If I wait, it might be too late." He swung up into the horse she'd finished saddling and spurred it forward. Dana grabbed the reins to stop him.

"I know I can't talk you out of going. Here, take this." She handed him the pistol he knew she kept in the barn. "It's loaded and ready to fire. Be careful." Her voice broke. "Help Mary."

He rode off up the road headed for the mountaintop. He knew where Mary would take Lucy. It was her favorite spot—and the most dangerous.

As he rode at a full-out gallop, he thought of his misgivings about Lucy. Fiona must have loved the fact that she'd fooled him. That she'd fooled them all, especially trusting Mary. The woman had known exactly how to worm her way into Mary's life, how to get her claws into her and make her believe that she was her friend.

What Fiona didn't know how to do was let go.

He took the trail, riding fast and hard, staying low in the saddle to avoid the pine tree limbs. His heart was in his throat, his fear for Mary a thunderous beat in his chest and his abhorrence for Fiona a bitter taste in his mouth. He prayed as he rode that he would reach them in time. That the woman Fiona had become would spare Mary who'd done nothing to her.

But he had little hope. He knew Fiona. She had come all the way to Montana to extract her vengeance. She'd become another person, Lucy, taking her time, playing Mary. Did she know that they were on to her? That's what frightened him the most. If she thought that Mary was turning against her or that the authorities knew…

MARY TURNED TO the woman in surprise, telling herself she must have heard wrong. "What did you just say?"

"I slept with Chase before you sent the letter."

She stared at the woman even as her heart began to pound. "What are you talking about?"

"I'm Fiona."

Mary took a step back as the woman she'd known as Lucy pulled a gun and pointed it at her heart.

Lucy laughed. "Surprise! I read your pathetic letter, and I hated you for taking him from me. You're the reason Chase broke up with me. Instead, the accident helped me become Lucy. You liked Lucy, didn't you? We could have been such good friends. But then Chase showed up—just as I knew he would."

Mary's mind was reeling. This was Lucy. And yet as she stared at her, she knew this was the woman who Chase said had tried to kill him before he left Arizona. The woman he'd said was delusional.

"You think you know him so well." Lucy shook her head. "I was in love with him. He and I were so good together. You don't want to believe that, do you? Well, it's true. There was something between us, something real and amazing, but then you wrote that letter." Lucy's face twisted in disgust. "You ruined my life. You ruined Chase's."

Mary was shaking her head, still having trouble believing this was happening. Chase had tried to warn her, but she'd thought she knew Lucy. She'd really thought she was a friend.

Until she'd taken a sip of the coffee this morning and tasted that horribly familiar chalky taste. "You drugged me."

Lucy shrugged. "You shouldn't have poured out your coffee this morning. That was really rude. I was nice enough to get it for you."

"You wanted to make me sick again?"

"I was being kind," Lucy said, looking confused. "This would have been so much easier if you'd been sick. Now, it's going to get messy." She jabbed the gun at her. "If you had just stayed mad at Chase, this wouldn't be happening either."

Mary didn't know what to say or do. She'd never

dealt with someone this unbalanced. "You want to make him suffer. Is that what this is about?"

Lucy smiled her gap-toothed smile. "For starters."

"You want him to fall in love with you again." She saw at once that was exactly what Lucy wanted. "But if you hurt me, that won't happen."

"It won't happen anyway and we both know it. Because of you." The woman sounded close to tears. "I could have made him happy. Before the letter came from you, he needed me. I could tell. He would have fallen in love with me."

Mary doubted that, but she kept the thought to herself. "If you hurt me, you will lose any chance you have for happiness."

Lucy laughed, sounding more like the woman she'd thought she knew. "Women like me don't find happiness. That's what my mother used to say. But then she let my stepfather and brothers physically and sexually abuse me."

Mary felt her heart go out to the woman despite the situation. "I'm so sorry. That's horrible. You deserved so much better."

Lucy laughed. "I took care of all of them, sending them to hell on earth, and for a while, I was happy, now that I think about it."

"Lucy—"

"Call me Fiona. I know how much you hate hearing that name. Fiona. Fiona. Fiona." She let out a high-pitched laugh that drowned out birdsong but not the thunder of hooves as a horse and rider came barreling across the mountaintop.

CHASE REINED IN his horse as all his fears were realized. The women had been standing at the edge of the mountaintop, Fiona holding a gun pointed at Mary's heart. But when they'd heard him coming, Fiona had grabbed Mary and pressed the muzzle of the weapon to her rival's throat.

"Nice you could join us," Fiona said as he slowly dismounted. "I wondered how long it would take before you realized who I was."

"I sensed it the first time I saw you," he said as he walked toward the pair, his gaze on Fiona and the gun. He couldn't bear to look into Mary's eyes. Fear and disgust. This was all his fault. He'd brought Fiona into their lives. Whatever happened, it was on him.

"I knew it was you," he said, and she smiled.

"It's the chemistry between us. When you pretended not to know me, well, that hurt, Chase. After everything we meant to each other…"

"Exactly," he said. "That's why you need to let Mary go. This is between you and me, Fiona."

Her face clouded. "Please, you think I don't know that you came riding up like that to save her?"

"Maybe I came to save you."

Fiona laughed, a harsh bitter sound. "Save me from what?"

"Yourself. Have any of the men you've known tried to save you, Fiona?" The question seemed to catch her off guard. "Did any of them care what happened to you?"

She met his gaze. "Don't pretend you care."

"I'm not pretending. I never wanted to hurt you. When I heard they found your car in the river, I was devastated. I didn't want things to end that way for you." He saw her weaken a little and took a step toward her and Mary.

"But you don't love me."

That was true and he knew better than to lie. "No. I'd already given away my heart when I met you. It wasn't fair, but it's the truth."

"But you picked me up at that party and brought me back to your place."

He shook his head as he took another step closer. "Rick asked you to drive me home because I'd had too much to drink."

She stared at him as if she'd told herself the story so many times, she didn't remember the truth. "But we made love."

"Did we? I remember you pulling off my boots and jeans right before I passed out."

Fiona let out a nervous laugh. "We woke up in the same bed."

"We did," he agreed as he stepped even closer. "But I suspect that's all that happened that night."

She swallowed and shook her head, tears welling in her eyes. "I liked you. I thought you and I—"

"But you knew better once I told you that I was in love with someone else."

"Still, if you had given us a chance." Fiona made a pleading sound.

"Let Mary go. She had nothing to do with what happened between us."

Fiona seemed to realize how close he was to the

two of them. She started to take a step back, dragging Mary along with her. The earth crumbled under her feet and she began to fall.

Chase could see that she planned to take Mary with her. He dived for the gun, for Mary, praying Fiona didn't pull the trigger as she fell. He caught Mary with one hand and reached for the gun barrel with the other. The report of the handgun filled the air as he yanked Mary forward, breaking Fiona's hold on her. But Mary still teetered on the sheer edge of the cliff as he felt a searing pain in his shoulder. His momentum had carried him forward. He shoved Mary toward the safety of the mountain top as was propelled over the edge of the drop-off.

He felt a hand grab his sleeve. He looked up to see Mary, clinging to him, determined not to let him fall.

Below him, he saw Fiona tumbling down the mountainside over boulders. Her body crashed into a tree trunk, but kept falling until it finally landed in a pile of huge rocks at the bottom.

As Mary helped pull him back up to safety, he saw that Fiona wasn't moving, her body a rag doll finally at rest. Behind them he heard horses. Pulling Mary to him, he buried his face in her neck, ignoring the pain in his shoulder as he breathed in the scent of her.

"He's shot," Chase heard Dana cry before everything went black.

Chapter Twenty

Chase opened his eyes to see Mary sitting next to his hospital bed as the horror of what had happened came racing back. "Are you—"

"I'm fine," she said quickly, and rose to reach for his hand. "How are you?"

He glanced down at the bandage on his shoulder. "Apparently, I'm going to live. How long have I been out?"

"Not long. You were rushed into surgery to remove the bullet. Fortunately, it didn't hit anything vital."

He stared into her beautiful blue eyes. "I was so worried about you. I'm so sorry."

She shook her head. "I should have listened to you."

Chase laughed. "I wouldn't make a habit of that."

"I'm serious. You tried to warn me."

He sobered. "This is all my fault."

"You didn't make her do the things she did." Her voice broke. Tears filled her eyes. "I thought we were both going to die. You saved my life."

"You saved mine," he said, and squeezed her hand. "Once I'm out of this bed—"

"Slow down, cowboy," the doctor said as he came into the room. "It will be a while before you get out of that bed."

"I need to get well soon, Doc. I'm going to marry this woman."

Mary laughed. "I think he's delirious," she joked, her cheeks flushed.

"I've never been more serious," he called after her as the doctor shooed her from the room. "I love that woman. I've always loved Mary Cardwell Savage," he called before the door closed. He was smiling as he lay back, even though the effort of sitting up had left him in pain. "I need to get well, Doc. I have to buy a ring."

HUD LEANED BACK in his office chair and read the note Fiona-Lucy had left in her apartment. That the woman had lived just a floor below his daughter still made his heart race with terror.

By the time, you find this, I will probably be dead. Or with luck, long gone. Probably dead because I'm tired of living this life. Anyway, I have nowhere to go. I came here to make Chase Steele pay for breaking my heart. Sometimes I can see that it wasn't him that made me do the things I've done. That it started long before him. It's the story of my life. It's the people who have hurt me. It's the desperation I feel to be like other people, happy, content, loved.

But there is an anger in me that takes over the rest of the time. I want to hurt people the way I've been hurt and much worse. I killed my mother, stepfather and stepbrothers in a fire. Since then, I've hurt other people who hurt me—and some who didn't. Some, like Deputy Dillon Ramsey, deserved to die. Christy Shores, not so much.

Today, I will kill a woman who doesn't deserve it in order to hurt a man who I could have loved if only he had loved me. He will die too. If not today, then soon. And then… I have no idea. I just know that I'm tired. I can't keep doing this.

Then again, I might feel differently tomorrow.

Hud carefully put the letter back into the evidence bag and sealed it. Fiona was gone. She'd died of her injuries after falling off the mountain. Because she had no family, her body would be cremated. Chase had suggested that her ashes be sent back to Arizona to her friend, Patty, the one person who'd stuck by her.

Two of his murders had been solved by the letter. The third, Grady Birch, was also about to be put to rest. A witness with a cabin not far from where Grady's body was found had come forward. He'd seen a man dragging what he now suspected was a body down to the river. That man had been Deputy Dillon Ramsey, who the witness identified after

Dillon's photo had run in the newspaper following his murder.

According to the law, everything would soon be neatly tied up, Hud thought as he put away the evidence bag. But crimes left scars. He could only hope that his daughter would be able to overcome hers. He had a feeling that Chase would be able to help her move on. He wouldn't mind a wedding out at the ranch. It had been a while, and he was thinking how much his wife loved weddings—and family—when his phone rang. It was Dana.

"I just got the oddest call from our son Hank," his wife said without preamble. "He says he's coming home for a visit and that he's bringing someone with him. A woman."

Hud could hear the joy in Dana's voice. "I told you that it would just take time, didn't I? This is great news."

"I never thought he'd get over Naomi," she said, but quickly brightened again. "I can't wait to meet this woman and see our son. It's been too long."

He couldn't have agreed more. "How's Mary?"

"She's picking up Chase at the hospital. Given the big smile on her face when she left the ranch, I'd say she's going to be just fine. How do you feel about a wedding or two in our future?"

He chuckled. "You just read my mind, but don't go counting your chickens before they hatch. Let's take it one at a time." But he found himself smiling as he hung up. Hank was coming home. He'd missed his son more than he could even tell Dana. He just hoped Hank really was moving on.

CHASE COULDN'T WAIT to see Mary. He was champing at the bit to get out of the hospital. He'd called a local jewelry store and had someone bring up a tray of engagement rings for him to choose one. He refused to put it off until he was released. The velvet box was in his pocket. Now he was only waiting for the nurse to wheel him down to the first floor—and Mary—since it was hospital policy, he'd been told.

Earlier, his father had stopped by. Chase had been glad to see him. Like his father, he'd made mistakes. They were both human. He'd been angry with a man who hadn't even known he existed. But he could understand why his mother had kept the truth from not only him, but also Jim Harris.

He didn't know what kind of relationship they could have, but he no longer felt as if there was a hole in his heart where a father should have been. Everyone said Jim was a good man who'd had some bad luck in his life. Chase couldn't hold that against him.

When his hospital room door opened, he heard the creak of the wheelchair and practically leaped off the bed in his excitement. He and Mary had been apart for far too long. He didn't want to spend another minute away from her. What they had was too special to let it go. He would never take their love for each for granted again.

To his surprise, it wasn't the nurse who brought in the wheelchair. "Mary?"

She looked different today. He was trying to put his finger on what it was when she grinned and shoved the wheelchair to one side as she approached.

MARY COULDN'T EXPLAIN the way she felt. But she was emboldened by everything that had happened. When Chase had first come back, she'd told herself that she couldn't trust him after he'd left Montana. But in her heart, she'd known better. Still, she'd pushed him away, letting her pride keep her from the man she loved.

Instead, she'd trusted Lucy. The red flags had been there, but she'd ignored them because she'd wanted to like her. She'd missed her friends who had moved away. She'd been vulnerable, and she'd let a psychopath into her life.

But now she was tired of being a victim, of not going after what she wanted. What she wanted was Chase.

She stepped to him, grabbed the collar of his Western shirt and pulled him into a searing kiss. She heard his intake of breath. The kiss had taken him by surprise. But also his shoulder was still healing.

"Oh, I'm so sorry," she said, drawing back, her face heating with embarrassment.

"I'm not," he said as he pulled her to him with his good arm and kissed her. When she drew back she started to say something, but she hushed him with a finger across his lips. "I have to know, Chase Steele. Are you going to be mine or not?"

He let out a bark of a laugh. "I've always been yours, Mary Savage."

She sighed and said, "Right answer."

His grin went straight to her heart. He pulled her close again and this time his kiss was fireworks. She melted into his arms. "Welcome home, Chase."

* * * * *

*The Cardwell Ranch: Montana Legacy series
by* New York Times *bestselling author
B.J. Daniels continues with Hank's Story.
Read on for a sneak peek.*

Hank Savage squinted into the sun glaring off the dirty windshield of his pickup as Cardwell Ranch came into view. He slowed the truck to a stop, resting one sun-browned arm over the top of the steering wheel as he took it all in.

The ranch, with its log and stone structures, didn't appear to have changed in the least. Nor had the two-story house where he'd grown up. Memories flooded him of hours spent on the back of a horse, of building forts in the woods around the creek, of the family sitting around the large table in the kitchen in the mornings, the sun pouring in, the sound of laughter. He saw and felt everything he'd given up, everything he'd run from, everything he'd lost.

"Been a while?" asked the sultry dark-haired woman in the passenger seat.

He nodded around the lump in his throat, shoved back his Stetson and wondered what the hell he was doing back here. This was a bad idea, probably his worst ever.

"Having second thoughts?" He'd warned Frankie about his big family, but she'd said she could handle it. He wasn't all that sure *he* could handle this. He prided himself on being fearless about most things. Give him a bull that hadn't been ridden, and he wouldn't hesitate to climb right on. Same with his job as a lineman. He'd faced gale winds hanging from a pole to get the power back on, braved getting fried more times than he liked to remember.

But coming back here, facing the past? He'd never been more afraid. He knew it was just a matter of time before he saw Naomi—just as he had in his dreams, in his nightmares. She was here, right where he'd left her, waiting for him as she had been for eight long years. Waiting for him to come back and make things right.

He looked over at Frankie. "You sure about this?"

She sat up straighter to take in the ranch and him, took a breath and let it out. "I am if you are. After all, this was your idea."

Like she had to remind him. "Then I suggest you slide over here." He patted the seat between them and she moved over, cuddling against him as he put his free arm around her. She felt small and fragile, certainly not strong enough for what was to come. For a moment, he almost changed his mind. It wasn't too late. He didn't have the right to involve her in his past.

"It's going to be okay," she said, and nuzzled his neck where his dark hair curled at his collar. "Trust me."

He pulled her closer and let his foot up off the brake. The pickup began to roll toward the ranch. It wasn't that he didn't trust Frankie. He just knew that it was only a matter of time before Naomi came to him, pleading with him to do what he should have done eight years ago. He felt a shiver even though the summer day was unseasonably warm.

I'm here.

* * * * *

Available August 2019 wherever
Harlequin books are sold.

COMING NEXT MONTH FROM

⬥ HARLEQUIN®
™

INTRIGUE

Available July 16, 2019

#1869 IRON WILL
Cardwell Ranch: Montana Legacy • by B.J. Daniels
Hank Savage is certain his girlfriend was murdered, so he hires private investigator Frankie Brewster to pretend to be his lover and help him find the killer. Before long, they are in over their heads...and head over heels.

#1870 THE STRANGER NEXT DOOR
A Winchester, Tennessee Thriller • by Debra Webb
After spending eight years in jail for a crime she didn't commit, Cecelia Winters is eager to find out who really killed her father, a religious fanatic and doomsday prepper. In order to discover the truth, she must work with Deacon Ross, a man who is certain Cecelia killed his mentor and partner.

#1871 SECURITY RISK
The Risk Series: A Bree and Tanner Thriller • by Janie Crouch
A few months ago, Tanner Dempsey saved Bree Daniels, but suddenly they find themselves back in danger when Tanner's past comes back to haunt the couple. Will the pair be able to stop the criminal before it's too late?

#1872 ADIRONDACK ATTACK
Protectors at Heart • by Jenna Kernan
When Detective Dalton Stevens follows his estranged wife, Erin, to the Adirondack Mountains in an effort to win her back, neither of them expects to become embroiled in international intrigue. Then they are charged with delivering classified information to Homeland Security.

#1873 PERSONAL PROTECTION
by Julie Miller
Ivan Mostek knows two things: someone wants him dead and a member of his inner circle is betraying him. With undercover cop Carly Valentine by his side, can he discover the identity of the traitor before it's too late?

#1874 NEW ORLEANS NOIR
by Joanna Wayne
Helena Cosworth is back in New Orleans to sell her grandmother's house. Suddenly, she is a serial killer's next target, and she is forced to turn to Detective Hunter Bergeron, a man she once loved and lost, for help. Together, will they be able to stop the elusive French Kiss Killer?

YOU CAN FIND MORE INFORMATION ON UPCOMING HARLEQUIN® TITLES, FREE EXCERPTS AND MORE AT WWW.HARLEQUIN.COM.

HICNM0719

Get 4 FREE REWARDS!

We'll send you 2 FREE Books plus 2 FREE Mystery Gifts.

Harlequin Intrigue® books feature heroes and heroines that confront and survive danger while finding themselves irresistibly drawn to one another.

FREE
Value Over
$20

YES! Please send me 2 FREE Harlequin Intrigue® novels and my 2 FREE gifts (gifts are worth about $10 retail). After receiving them, if I don't wish to receive any more books, I can return the shipping statement marked "cancel." If I don't cancel, I will receive 6 brand-new novels every month and be billed just $4.99 each for the regular-print edition or $5.74 each for the larger-print edition in the U.S., or $5.74 each for the regular-print edition or $6.49 each for the larger-print edition in Canada. That's a savings of at least 12% off the cover price! It's quite a bargain! Shipping and handling is just 50¢ per book in the U.S. and 75¢ per book in Canada.* I understand that accepting the 2 free books and gifts places me under no obligation to buy anything. I can always return a shipment and cancel at any time. The free books and gifts are mine to keep no matter what I decide.

Choose one: ☐ **Harlequin Intrigue®**
Regular-Print
(182/382 HDN GMYW)

☐ **Harlequin Intrigue®**
Larger-Print
(199/399 HDN GMYW)

Name (please print)

Address   Apt. #

City   State/Province   Zip/Postal Code

Mail to the **Reader Service:**
IN U.S.A.: P.O. Box 1341, Buffalo, NY 14240-8531
IN CANADA: P.O. Box 603, Fort Erie, Ontario L2A 5X3

Want to try 2 free books from another series? Call 1-800-873-8635 or visit www.ReaderService.com.

---

*Terms and prices subject to change without notice. Prices do not include sales taxes, which will be charged (if applicable) based on your state or country of residence. Canadian residents will be charged applicable taxes. Offer not valid in Quebec. This offer is limited to one order per household. Books received may not be as shown. Not valid for current subscribers to Harlequin Intrigue books. All orders subject to approval. Credit or debit balances in a customer's account(s) may be offset by any other outstanding balance owed by or to the customer. Please allow 4 to 6 weeks for delivery. Offer available while quantities last.

Your Privacy—The Reader Service is committed to protecting your privacy. Our Privacy Policy is available online at www.ReaderService.com or upon request from the Reader Service. We make a portion of our mailing list available to reputable third parties that offer products we believe may interest you. If you prefer that we not exchange your name with third parties, or if you wish to clarify or modify your communication preferences, please visit us at www.ReaderService.com/consumerschoice or write to us at Reader Service Preference Service, P.O. Box 9062, Buffalo, NY 14240-9062. Include your complete name and address.

HI19R2

SPECIAL EXCERPT FROM

(H) HARLEQUIN

I N T R I G U E

*Three years ago, Deputy Tanner Dempsey was involved
in a mission that went wrong. Now, trying to keep his
PTSD under control while he falls deeper for
Bree Daniels, his past returns, threatening the life he
thought was finally back on track...*

Read on for a sneak peek at
Security Risk,
from USA TODAY *bestselling author Janie Crouch.*

It wasn't long before they were arriving at the ranch. He
grabbed her overnight bag, and they walked inside.

"We both need to get a few hours' sleep," he said. "I'll
take the couch and you can have the bed."

She walked toward the bedroom but turned at the
door. "Come with me. Just to sleep together like before."
Those big green eyes studied him as she reached her hand
out toward him.

There was nothing he wanted more than to curl up
with her in his bed. But with his anger and frustration so
close to the surface, he couldn't discount the fact that he
might wake up swinging. The thought of Bree being the
recipient of his night terrors made him break out into a
cold sweat.

"Never mind," she said quickly, misreading his hesitation,
hand falling back to her side. "You don't have to."

Damn it, he'd rather never sleep again than see that wounded look in her eyes from something he'd done.

He stepped toward her. "I want to. Trust me, there's nothing I want more. But…I just don't want to take a chance on waking you up if I get called back in to Risk Peak early." That was at least a partial truth.

The haunted look fell away from her eyes, and a shy smile broke on her face. "I don't mind. I'll take a shorter amount of sleep if it means I get to sleep next to you."

He would have given her anything in the world to keep that sweet smile on her face. He took her hand, and they walked into the bedroom together.

They took turns changing into sleep clothes in the bathroom, then got into the bed together. The act was so innocent and yet so intimate.

Tanner rolled over onto his side and pulled Bree's back against his front. He breathed in the sweet scent of her hair as her head rested in the crook of his elbow. His other arm wrapped loosely around her waist.

She was out within minutes, her smaller body relaxing against him, trusting him to shelter and protect her while she slept. Tanner wouldn't betray that trust, even if that meant protecting her against himself.

Besides, sleeping was overrated when he could be awake and feeling every curve that had been haunting his dreams for months pressed against him.

Definitely worth it.

Don't miss
Security Risk *by Janie Crouch,*
available August 2019 wherever
Harlequin® *Intrigue books and ebooks are sold.*

www.Harlequin.com

HIEXP0719

SPECIAL EXCERPT FROM

In order to clean up his player reputation, rodeo champ
and cowboy Nico Laramie asks his best friend,
Eden Joslin, to pretend they're an exclusive couple.
But one kiss with the woman he's always kept at a
distance and Nico knows this fake relationship is about
to turn into something very real...

Read on for a sneak peak at
Sweet Summer Sunset
part of the Coldwater Texas series from
USA TODAY bestselling author Delores Fossen.

"You've been avoiding me," Eden added, and she set the grocery bags on the small kitchen counter.

"I have," he admitted, and he wanted to wince. This was the problem with crossing a line with a friend. He wasn't used to putting on mouth filters when it came to Eden. "I wanted to give us both some time."

Her eyebrow came up, and she huffed before she mumbled some frustrated profanity under her breath.

"See?" he snapped, as if that proved all the arguments going on in his head. "We're uncomfortable with each other, and it's all because of the kiss that shouldn't have happened."

She stared at him a moment, caught on to a handful of his shirt and yanked him to her. She kissed him. Hard.

Nico felt his body jolt, an involuntary reaction that nearly made him dive in for more. After all, good kisses should be deep and involve some tongue. It was like stripping off a layer of clothes or going to the next level. But those were places that Nico stopped himself from going. Before their tongues could get involved, he stepped back from her, and she let go of him, her grip melting off his shirt.

He felt the loss right away when her mouth was no longer on his. The loss and the realization that Eden was a real, live, breathing woman. An attractive one with breasts, legs and everything.

Oh man.

He didn't want to realize that. He wanted his friend. And he wanted that friendship almost as much as he wanted to French-kiss her.

"Now we can also be uncomfortable because of that kiss I just gave you," she said, as if that proved whatever point she'd been trying to make. It proved nothing. Well, nothing that should be proved anyway.

Nico stared at her. "Eden, you're playing with a thousand gallons of fire," he warned her—after he'd caught his breath.

"I know, and I'm going to be honest about that. In fact, I'm going to insist we be honest with each other so that we don't ruin our friendship."

That was very confusing, and Nico wondered if this was some kind of trick. Except Eden wasn't a trick-playing kind of person. "What the heck do you mean by that?"

Her gaze stayed level with his. "It means if you want to kiss me, you should. If you don't want to kiss me again, then don't."

He was still confused. About what she was saying anyway. Nico was reasonably sure that the wanting-to-kiss-her part was highly charged right now.

"I just don't want you to avoid me because you're struggling with this possible curveball that's been tossed into our friendship," Eden went on. "That kiss makes us even," she added with a firm nod.

Don't miss
Sweet Summer Sunset *by Delores Fossen,*
available July 2019 wherever HQN books
and ebooks are sold.

www.Harlequin.com